A FRIEND OF THE FAMILY

Tina and Steve are rich, good looking and have everything they could want except a child of their own. Steve wants to develop his stately home as a garden centre and leisure complex. The lynchpin to this enterprise is Louise who has loyally worked for him for a number of years. Louise and Tina are complete opposites, both in looks and personality. Louise thinks Steve has married the wrong woman and should have realised that she would have been the perfect partner. Her obsession with Steve, her wish to be more closely bound to him, leads her to suggest that she should be a surrogate mother to his much wanted child by Tina. The consequences of this offer and the effect it has on the relationships not only of the three people most intimately concerned, but also their family and friends, is the subject of this riveting novel.

A FRIEND OF THE FAMILY

Nicola Thorne

CHIVERS PRESS
BATH

First published 2002
by
HarperCollins*Publishers*
This Large Print edition published by
Chivers Press
by arrangement with
HarperCollins*Publishers*
2002

ISBN 0 7540 9114 7

British Library Cataloguing in Publication Data available

Printed and bound in Great Britain by
BOOKCRAFT, Midsomer Norton, Somerset

This book is dedicated, with love, to my friend

CHAPTER ONE

'Had a nice day?'

'Very nice.' William scrambled into the seat beside Louise while his sister, Bethany, got into the back. 'How's Tina?'

'A bit better,' Louise said, pulling away from the kerb. 'I checked just before I left.' She drove cautiously along the road outside the school because the children emerging were sometimes apt to dash across the road without looking. William and Bethany's stepmother had one of her attacks of migraine which meant that she spent all day in a darkened room, sometimes as often as once or twice a week. She was not a strong woman but when she was well she did the school run. However, on the occasions when she wasn't, Louise filled in instead.

Louise liked filling in, doing these little jobs for Tina. It made her feel indispensable and, indeed, she was, both to Tina and her husband, the children's father Steve Lockwood.

While the children prattled to each other about the day's events Louise kept her eyes on the road, her mind on nothing in particular except, maybe, a niggling sense of resentment about Tina: it was always there, somewhere in the background, carefully under wraps, the fact that Tina had grabbed the man she'd wanted for herself.

Tina was an ex-model, half Swedish, tall, languid, aristocratic and undoubtedly sexy. So it was not hard to see why Steve had made this awful mistake. He'd been bewitched. However, she was also, in Louise's opinion, selfish, capricious, temperamental and a hypochondriac, qualities that Steve, blinded by love, either didn't notice or ignored. Like Steve, Tina too had been married before, the sort of woman who would never, could never, be without a man.

Louise on the other hand was solid, and independent-minded. She was not bad looking: tall, strong featured, fresh faced, vivacious, with curly brown hair. In looks, manner and personality she was the complete antithesis of Tina: dependable, vigorous, hard working, blessed with rude good health. This resentment that Steve had chosen Tina instead of her Louise tried to keep firmly under control, maintaining a façade to the world which, in many ways, she by now largely believed herself.

What she *did* have was the strong conviction that one day Steve would realise he had married the wrong woman. It would take time but it would happen. She was certain of that.

The children's school was a ten-mile drive from their home, Poynton Manor, a wonderful old house set in fifty acres of fertile countryside on the Dorset/Somerset border. The house had originally been built in the fifteenth century, but it had been gutted by fire several times and scarcely any part of the original building remained except possibly the walled garden where fruit, vegetables and flowers were grown that were sold in the shop.

Parts of the grounds were open to the public but the house wasn't. It stood well back from the shop and commercial garden complex and had its own secluded area of garden, surrounded by a large wall protecting it from the influx of visitors, especially the hordes which descended upon Poynton in the summer months.

Under the care of Duncan the head gardener it specialised in rare and exotic plants and attracted visitors from all over the country.

The car swept up the drive, stopped in front of the house and the children got out.

'Aren't you coming in to see Tina?' Bethany paused, half in, half out of the car.

Louise shook her head.

'I think you'd better leave her for a while. She felt very sick this morning.'

Bethany grimaced but didn't seem very concerned. They were a bit offhand about their stepmother in the way she was offhand about them. They juggled both sets of parents, Tina and Steve, Frances and her new husband George, cleverly and satisfactorily. The result was that they were never without a home, parental concern—each set desiring to outdo the other in manifestations of affection and, of course, lots of presents.

Louise saw the children into the house and drove back along the drive to the shop, a complex about half a mile away, where she parked the car.

She was very fond of the children. She had been with them for six years which was a great part of their lives. Bethany had been four and William two when their mother, Frances, deserted them and Steve for another man.

Not long afterwards Louise left her secretarial job in London to take care of her sick mother who had a cottage on the Poynton estate. She began to help out in the estate office which meant helping to sort out Steve's complicated life. As well as his large house with its thriving farm he had global business interests and a peripatetic way of life which was probably why Frances had had enough of him.

There had been a small shop attached to the farm in a ramshackle building next to the greenhouses housing the rare plants. She and Duncan had managed it themselves and, gradually, Louise had introduced other items: honey from a local hive, herbs, boxes of organic vegetables including asparagus in season. Steve had entered enthusiastically into the scheme and suggested rebuilding. Architects were summoned and ambitious plans drawn up. Capable Louise was put in sole charge of development, ordering new stock: china and cut glass, ornaments, vases, tea-sets, dinner services. The Lockwoods were not a noble family, but Poynton had a long and noble history and many of the items were engraved with its coat of arms.

The new complex was to embrace a tea room and loos. Steve gave Louise free rein and a generous budget to spend on it. Those were such heady days, designing the shop, getting planning permission, innovations all over the place, a new car park, someone to run the tea room. Steve approved of everything she did, made valuable suggestions. They would often huddle over plans in the evening, facing each other across the kitchen table with a steak each and a bottle of wine between them.

Steve had gradually come to consult her on many other things besides the development of the estate, drawing her into his life more and more: a school for the children, their welfare requirements, stock for the shop, plans for a riding school. He would walk her home and kiss her lightly on the cheek when they said goodnight. It was inevitable

4

that, in time, Louise would come to feel that she was in love with him and, by his attention, his habit of telephoning her at all hours, his obvious need of her, he encouraged her to think he might feel the same.

But somehow that invitation never came, the intimacy she so longed for never developed. She convinced herself that, inevitably, it would, that he was still recovering from the shock of losing Frances, that wayward, obviously unstable wife with whom he had been deeply in love.

One had to understand, be patient, nurse a man through a crisis like that.

But the real shock came when, one day, Steve arrived home with Tina as a house guest, and it transpired he hadn't been grieving for Frances at all but had been courting a woman who was the complete opposite of the ex-wife, in looks and disposition, and a few months later he married her.

Louise nearly decided to pack it all in and go to Australia, but she stayed. She was too attached to the shop, the way of life at Poynton, to Bethany and William and, of course, to Steve.

*   *   *

It was a beautiful day, early spring, the waters of the stream beside the old mill sparkling as it rushed over the smooth pebbles lying on the bed. The herd of prize redhorn cows grazed contentedly in the field on the other side. In the distance was the house, a long drive winding up to it, so graceful and elegant in the spring sunshine.

The new, or by now almost new, shop complex with its doors open invitingly lay ahead, and there

5

were already several cars showing that even in early spring a good crowd of visitors had been attracted to look around for border plants, rare species for their greenhouses and, perhaps afterwards, take a Dorset cream tea in the café next door.

Louise parked the car, looked around her with a feeling of satisfaction at all she had accomplished since she'd been at Poynton, and made her way into the shop. To her surprise Tina was at the till checking in some items purchased by a couple of visitors. Louise stood beside her, silently helping to put the goods into the colourful carrier bags with the Poynton crest on the side. Then she handed them to the customers, a man and a woman who seemed very satisfied with their purchases and turned away with broad smiles.

'Are you sure you're up to this?' Louise looked at Tina who nodded.

'I'm much better. It wasn't the usual migraine. I just woke this morning feeling terribly nauseous.' She seemed preoccupied and started checking items that had registered on the till, a frown on her face. 'Our turnover is not as good as last year. Maybe we should cut down on some of the items.' Arms akimbo she wandered into the middle of the by now deserted shop floor. 'These dinner services hardly move.'

'They're so lovely.' Louise gazed at them wistfully, plates of the finest porcelain retailing at twenty-five pounds each. The full dinner service was nearly a thousand pounds.

'But if it doesn't sell, it's taking up room.' Tina started going round the various stands writing in the notebook she carried in her hand.

Louise watched her, her emotions the usual mix

6

of envy, resentment and disdain. Despite her lack of experience, her complete ignorance either of rare plants or merchandising, once she was Mrs Lockwood Tina had taken over. As a jet-setter who had moved around the world as much as Steve she seemed to think she knew it all.

Besides, she soon grew bored with country life in Poynton and took little notice of the children. She went up to London and abroad on buying trips, returning with orders for merchandise which, when it arrived, was exquisite but proved very hard to sell.

It had been Tina's decision to go so upmarket. Now she made it sound as though it was Louise's fault that they had surplus stock on their hands. This was unfair because Louise had been more realistic. She knew the market. After the arrival of Tina everything changed, but she was Steve's wife and Steve paid her wages.

Although there had been no more late dinners in the kitchen, Louise felt that there was still the same sense of regard for her, his appreciation of what she did for the business, the family and the children, and now a concern for delicate Tina and her frequent bouts of ill health. There was the feeling that Steve relied on his robust, reliable helpmeet and that he always would.

A new wave of customers emerged from the garden entrance clutching a variety of plants in pots. More people came in through the main entrance, and gradually the shop filled up again. Louise took over at the till and Tina disappeared with her list into the stock-room.

What was left of the rest of the afternoon was busy. At five-thirty Louise saw the last customer out, stood for a few moments watching the cars depart and then went back into the shop and locked the door.

She returned to the till to cash up thinking that by now Tina must have returned to the house. She finished cashing up, locked the till and was about to turn off the lights when she noticed that the door to the stock-room still had a light under it. She went across, opened the door and saw Tina lying on the ground.

For a moment Louise stood transfixed, sure that Tina was dead. Then she rushed to her side, knelt down and saw that she was still breathing.

Tina opened her eyes.

'I think I fainted,' she murmured. 'I've been lying here for some time.'

'Can you move? Are you alright?'

Tina was young, but was it possible she had suffered a stroke?

Louise prodded her carefully while Tina tried to sit upright and finally managed it. She sat for a while, her head in her hands. 'I felt terribly whoozy.'

'You should have called me. I'll call Steve.'

'You'll have to try and get him on his mobile. I've no idea where he is.' Tina made a renewed attempt to get to her feet, swayed again and collapsed once more on Louise.

'You'd better sit down,' Louise said, leading her to a chair in the corner.

'I think I hurt my knee when I fell.' Tina was limping badly, one foot seemingly unable to touch the ground. Reaching the chair she sat down heavily.

'I feel I should call the doctor first.' Louise had

begun to feel a little frightened.

'No, call Steve,' Tina said imperiously. 'It's nothing. It will pass.'

Leaving her on the chair Louise went into the shop and dialled Steve's mobile but only got the answering service. She hesitated, looked into the stock-room again and then across to the greenhouses where she saw Duncan rearranging his plants, filling in gaps where purchases had been made.

Louise hurried through the connecting doors.

'Duncan,' she called, 'can you give me a hand with Tina? She's not well.'

'Oh!' Duncan, a monosyllabic Scotsman, raised his head. 'Did you call the doctor?'

'She wants Steve but I can't get him on the phone. Can you help me get her into the house and into bed?'

'Do what I can.' Duncan dolefully shook his head and followed Louise across the floor of the shop into the stock-room. Tina was now sitting upright and Louise thought some colour had returned to her face.

'I *think* I'm alright,' she said, getting slowly to her feet. 'Honestly.' She gave a wan smile. 'A bit shaky, but I think I can get up to the house.'

'I'll take you in the car,' Louise volunteered. 'It's just outside.'

Leaving Tina with Duncan, Louise ran across to the car and drove it up to the main door of the shop by which time Tina, Duncan by her side, stood waiting for her.

'Will you be alright now?' Duncan peered into the car.

'I really am very much better. I don't know what

came over me.'

'Aftermath of the headache,' Louise said waving to Duncan as she turned the car. 'You got up too early.'

'I get this awful nausea. It comes over me in waves.'

'I still think you should see the doctor.'

Tina shook her head. 'I'll be OK once I lie down for a bit. Are the children alright?'

'They're fine.'

Tina nodded abstractedly. The housekeeper, Mrs Barton, usually gave the children their tea and settled them down to their homework. She lived with her husband, who ran the farm, in one of the cottages on the estate.

By the time they reached the house Tina seemed quite capable of making her own way, but slowly, and Louise followed her through the main door, across the large hall and up the stairs to the first floor and the master suite at the end with its lovely views over the lake and surrounding countryside. Steve's room. Louise always felt a tiny frisson when she entered it which was quite often with Tina's frequent bouts of ill health.

The bedroom with its king-sized bed was huge, gracious, carpeted in pale grey Wilton. It had built-in cupboards on one side, wardrobes on the other, a writing desk and some easy chairs drawn up to the French windows which led onto a balcony. The windows were draped with a heavy, rich Liberty fabric; large fantastic bird-like creatures, blue, orange and red against a soft grey background. The walls and woodwork were white and there was no central light but lamps on tables on either side of the bed and dotted throughout the room, and a standard lamp illuminating the desk in a wall embrasure.

Off the bedroom was the bathroom and next door Steve's dressing room.

'I'll try Steve again.' Louise went over to the phone by the bed but, again, there was no answer. Tina had disappeared into the bathroom where Louise could hear the distressing sounds of retching which went on for several seconds. Finally Tina staggered back into the bedroom, this time dressed in a white bathrobe.

'God, I feel terrible,' she said, collapsing onto the bed, her face covered with tiny beads of sweat.

'I really am going to call the doctor,' Louise said firmly. 'I wouldn't want to be held responsible if anything happened to you.'

'Oh, nothing will happen to me,' Tina laughed weakly. 'Basically I am perfectly robust. I think you're right, I got up too early. I feel fine while I'm lying down.' She looked across at Louise and gave her a tremulous smile.

'Please don't call Dr Hunter. He'll just give me stronger pills.' She closed her eyes and sighed wearily.

'I'll make you a cup of tea.' Louise perched on the side of the bed next to Tina and sat for a moment looking critically at her. Really Tina was so wretchedly, undeniably beautiful, with those china blue eyes, pale skin and naturally blonde hair. Yet there was something so false about her. One even doubted that her illness was real. It was looks and looks alone, Louise was sure, which had made Steve choose Tina instead of her.

However, Tina most certainly was far from robust. She always had something wrong with her.

She was always off to London to consult a specialist for some unspecified ailment. Louise thought that this inevitably played on Steve's emotions leaving him with a constant feeling of insecurity; an urge always to be on call in case Tina needed him, as she had today: the frail woman in need of a strong man.

Tina had opened her eyes and Louise leaned towards her.

'Tina, I know it's none of my business,' she began hesitantly. 'But . . . could you be pregnant? I mean the symptoms . . .'

Tina put a hand feebly against her brow. 'If only,' she sighed deeply. 'That's part of the trouble. I can't have a baby. I've had all the tests. It will never happen. If only it would.'

And then she started to weep quietly and Louise, rather shocked by the announcement, couldn't think of any way to help her other than by patting her shoulder and murmuring, 'There, there.'

'I think I've failed Steve.' Tina reached beneath the pillow for a tissue and began to dry her eyes.

'But Steve has two children.'

'That's the point. We'd like a family of our own. Steve hates it in the holidays when the children go to stay with their mother. He feels they're only half his. And I feel I'm only half a wife because I can't give him what he wants.'

Leaving Tina a short while afterwards to sleep again Louise pondered on her words and the strange situation she had revealed. Tina showed such scant interest in Bethany and William, why would she possibly want children of her own?

When Steve came down Louise stood by the Aga looking anxiously at him. 'How is she?'

'Asleep. Thank goodness. The doctor gave her a sedative.'

'But there's nothing seriously wrong?'

Steve shook his head.

'Low blood pressure, that and the migraine.'

'She said she was nauseous.'

'That's part of the migraine. That and other things.'

The doctor had been summoned as soon as Steve came home and arrived soon afterwards. Everyone fussed about Tina, as though she had them all on a fine thread that could easily snap. Even she, Louise, who could see through her, fussed about Tina.

'I was going to take her some supper.'

Steve shook his head.

'Don't bother. She says she'll only bring it up.'

He looked at the single place laid on the kitchen table.

'Won't you have something too, Louise?'

'If you like.' Louise stared at the casserole simmering on the stove.

'Of course I like.' Steve poured a glass of wine from the bottle standing on the table. 'Get a glass and have one yourself.'

With Tina he would have jumped up and done it for her. With Louise it wasn't necessary. But it didn't matter. She felt excited, almost elated. This was how it used to be: cosy suppers in the kitchen after a hard day's work. Louise began dishing out a plate of casserole and vegetables which she set before him.

'Just like old times,' she said lightly, but her words or their meaning didn't seem to register. Steve looked tired and drawn. She worried about him, much more than she worried about Tina.

Steve was forty with corn-coloured hair streaked with grey which he wore rather long. He had large, luminous, deeply recessed blue eyes, a lean and cavernous face. He was a tall, taut, wiry man with an air of restless energy that made him very attractive to women. He always wore casual clothes, open-necked, hand-made shirts and well-cut bespoke jackets and trousers. Louise had never seen him in a suit, and he seldom wore a tie.

Aroused from his reverie Steve said, 'Are the children OK?'

'They're watching TV.'

'They should be in bed.'

'I'll see to that after supper.'

'You're very good.' He looked at her fondly. 'But I'll put the kids to bed. I don't see enough of them. Believe me, I am grateful. I don't know what we'd do without you. You're a brick.'

Louise frowned. She didn't like the 'we'. What he meant was that he didn't know what he'd do without her. Neither did she. She was essential to him. Why was it taking Steve so long to realise this?

Steve poured himself another glass of wine, didn't bother with a glass for her and tucked into the plate set before him. Louise also helped herself, poured a glass of wine and sat down opposite him.

'Tina and I had a little chat this afternoon,' she said conversationally. 'She kind of opened her heart out to me. I was touched.' Louise looked

14

hesitantly at Steve. 'About wanting a baby. It explains why Tina goes to London so often to see the doctors. I thought it was her migraine.'

Steve looked up, grunted and resumed eating. Clearly he was hungry, maybe a little embarrassed too.

'So, she told you?' he murmured after a while.

'I'm very sorry.'

'She wants a baby so much. She thinks of little else. It has become an obsession.' His gaze as he looked at Louise was troubled. 'I've offered to try and adopt, but it's not the same.' He sat back and sighed. 'She wants *our* baby.'

'She told me it was for you.' Louise was aware that she had to guard her reaction, not appear jealous or petulant. She had, for the moment, to be a buddy to Tina as well as Steve, to enjoy the confidence of both. 'But I can't understand why she wants children when . . .' she paused.

'When what?' Steve looked puzzled.

'Well . . . with Bethany and William . . . she's not exactly devoted.'

'Oh!' Steve protested, 'Tina is *very* fond of them. But it is not the same as children of your own. Of course I understand that. This has become important for her. The thing is that I love her so much I'd do anything to make her happy. Can you see that Lou?' he gazed at her earnestly.

Louise didn't reply.

After they'd eaten she cleared up while he sat back smoking a cigarette.

Then he got up and after another brief word of thanks he went off to see Tina, and Louise found her own way home, alone.

15

CHAPTER TWO

The woman recounted how she had babies for infertile couples. She seemed to make a habit of it. She was thirty-five and had never had children of her own. She admitted that she always felt a wrench about giving them up. It was difficult to make out the motivation of someone for this sort of behaviour. Louise grew more and more puzzled as she watched the documentary.

It was an area full of pitfalls. One woman refused to hand over her baby to the couple, even though the man had fathered the child. A legal case had followed.

Louise watched the programme to the end, turned it off and went to bed.

But that night she was very restless, tossing and turning in bed, sleeping only briefly, to wake up again. The TV programme about surrogacy seemed unsettling, to assume a dominant place in her mind. Inevitably she supposed she linked it with the recent news about Tina being unable to have children.

It was market day so at five Louise got up to make a cup of tea. Her cat Morgan eagerly followed her down to the kitchen, relishing the prospect of an early breakfast. Louise fed Morgan and let him out, standing for a while at the back door listening to the familiar sounds of the country, inhaling the fresh morning air.

Nether Poynton was a hamlet which at one time had consisted entirely of people whose function it was to serve and support the manor. In many ways it hadn't changed very much. Most of the dwellings were still occupied by those who worked on the estate, though there were a few cottages which were used at the weekends by city folk from Bristol or further afield. Her mother had bought a cottage there after her father, a businessman in Bristol, succumbed early to a heart attack brought on by overwork. She had been one of the few long-term residents not connected with the manor.

The Poynton family had died out when Douglas Poynton, the heir, and his two younger brothers had been killed in the Great War, leaving a bereaved and widowed mother, the sole survivor of a once large and loving family. On her death the estate had been sold, much of it broken up, and in the years until Steve Lockwood bought it it had belonged to a variety of owners, few of whom had done anything to maintain it, and sold off most of the properties belonging to it.

Steve, a wealthy London businessman, had bought it on his marriage to Frances and with the enthusiasm with which he did everything set about restoring it with the intention of starting a dynasty of his own. When properties became vacant he tried to buy them back. He reorganised and extended the home farm, put Geoffrey Barton in to run it, and he spent a fortune on restoring the house to its original Elizabethan glory.

When Frances deserted him the work was just completed and he had done too much to turn his back on all his efforts.

That was eight years ago, and it was soon after that that Louise, who had left London to take care of her ailing mother, joined him.

Two years later her mother died leaving Louise

a pleasant, roomy cottage within sight of the big house, plus a small inheritance. The job gave Louise, burdened with the care of a sick mother, a lifeline and, as it turned out, she gave one to Steve.

After making her tea Louise didn't feel like going back to bed. It looked like being a pleasant day.

Buddy came around six-thirty to take her to market in Yeovil, his van full of fresh produce which he sold on his stall. Louise didn't stay with him but wandered round the town doing some shopping and seeing what else was in the market. Sometimes she got ideas for the shop at Poynton though less of these after Tina took over.

Louise put on the television in the kitchen and pottered about clearing up, thinking of the supper with Steve, the events of the previous day. He'd stayed in the kitchen quite a long time, at ease with her, more relaxed than when he'd come in, lingering over his cigarette and talking to her before going to join his wife.

Tina was beautiful, but that beauty would fade, was already fading, as often happens with very attractive women. After thirty they went downhill and Tina was thirty-five. She had absolutely no talents or attainments and was frequently ill. She was moody and given to going to London or Paris on spending sprees, bringing home a whole lot of clothes that she would wear once or twice, or not at all. How Steve must have despaired. But his nobility of character was such that he was very loyal to Tina, seldom complaining, though very occasionally he was heard to mutter under his breath about her extravagance and then give a deprecating laugh, as though conscious of having

18

made a joke.

Louise finished her tea, completed her tidying, had a bath and was dressed and eating breakfast just after six.

Buddy usually had a cup of tea and then they set off to reach the market site shortly before seven.

Buddy Grant wanted to marry Louise despite what he called her obsession with Steve. She was irritated when he used this term because it certainly was not. It sounded as though she was crazy and she wasn't. She was perfectly sane. He said Steve gave her no encouragement, no hope. She was wasting her time.

She had known Buddy since she came to Nether Poynton to take care of Mother. Before she'd arrived he'd been good to Mother and drove her to the hospital. He was a very kind, considerate man, slightly younger than she was, amiable, likeable, but to her nothing more. Buddy was to her what she was to Steve: indispensable. It was a similar kind of relationship, a fact that she frequently pointed out to Buddy which put him in a quandary because Louise gave him no encouragement either.

As she looked at the clock to check the time she heard the sound of Buddy's van and jumping up reached for her anorak as he pushed open the door and popped his head round.

'Time for a cup of tea?' she asked.

'No thanks,' he shook his head. 'I'm a bit late today. Overslept.'

Louise nodded, shrugged her arms into her anorak, checked that the cat flap in the back door was open and followed him out.

Buddy was a large, thick-set man with the build of a rugby player. He captained the local team. It was impossible not to like him, he was so good natured. It was a pity she couldn't love him in the way he said he loved her. Life would have been so much less complicated. But it was good that he was not connected with Poynton Manor and all that went on there, so much so that it was really ninety-five per cent of her life. It was useful to have some outside interest, otherwise the atmosphere of that close-knit community was almost claustrophobic.

However, the first thing he did when they got going was to ask how Tina was.

'I heard she wasn't well.'

Louise looked at him in surprise.

'How did you hear that?'

'I had a drink in the pub with Duncan. He said she fainted in the stock-room.'

'She's got low blood pressure.' Louise sounded offhand. She looked at Buddy and smiled. 'She's not going to die if that's what you're thinking.'

'I wasn't thinking that at all,' Buddy protested, peering through the early morning light, but he could almost have made his way blindfolded. He looked forward to these weekly jaunts with Louise with a peculiar feeling of excitement despite their regularity. In a way he supposed he was as obsessed with her as she was with Steve. Because she was unattainable he wanted her all the more. Yet there was no real barrier to a relationship between them as there was for her with Steve, so his attitude was not as illogical as Louise's. She was free. Steve was not.

In many ways he thought he and Louise were so compatible. They were both of a practical turn of mind, loved the countryside and outdoor life. In everything except her attitude to Steve, Louise was sensible, straightforward and uncomplicated. He found her robust good looks very attractive. She had no foibles, no airs and graces like Tina. Why then was she wasting her life on a man like Steve? There were so many things they could do; they could have such a good life together if only . . . Buddy glanced at her sideways.

'What do you think about women who have babies for infertile couples?' Louise, chin resting in the palm of her hand, looked sharply at him. 'Do you think they're crazy?'

'It's something I've never thought about,' Buddy said, taken aback.

'There was a programme last night on the telly about surrogate mothers. You wonder why they do it.'

'For money I suppose.'

'I suppose.' Louise looked thoughtful. 'But there doesn't seem to be much money in it. Not in this country anyway. One woman has had five children and given them all away. Fancy carrying a baby for nine months, just to do that.'

'It doesn't sound natural to me.' Buddy shook his head. Such a concept, such behaviour, was completely beyond his comprehension. 'Does it bother you?' he asked, looking again at Louise.

'No.' She took her hand away from her chin and shook her head. 'Not at all. Just thinking.'

By now they were on the outskirts of Yeovil, joined by early morning commuter traffic and other vans and lorries making their way to market.

When they got to the site Louise helped Buddy unload his van and set up his stall. They shared coffee from a thermos and as the shops began to open and customers converged on the market place she made her farewell and wandered up through the town.

*   *   *

Yeovil was not exactly a pretty town. It was lacking in old-world charm, yet it was attractively set on the Dorset/Somerset border and surrounded by tree-topped hills with cattle grazing on the slopes. Everywhere there was a reminder that this was a rural market town whose fortunes ebbed and flowed with the income of those who used it. Mainly they were farmers and people whose living depended on the country.

Just as the twentieth century had drawn to its close the farming community had been hit by a tremendous crisis which caused a brain disease in cattle and the fear that this could be transferred to human beings. Thousands of farmers who'd had to have their cattle slaughtered had had their livelihoods drastically reduced. Many had lost them altogether. Some had taken their own lives. Rural England was in crisis.

But the economy of the town of Yeovil depended not solely on farmers and those who earned their living on the land. On its outskirts was a giant helicopter group employing many hundreds of people who were independent of the land.

In addition, the beauty of Dorset, combined with its relative accessibility, made it a very attractive county to Londoners wishing to have a second home away from the metropolis, or to those who had retired from business or, in particular, the armed services. Yeovil was where these mainly well-off people did their shopping now that the

22

shops in so many villages had closed.

Yeovil had a large, traffic-free precinct called The Quedam and two main streets full of shops. It was built on a hill and from almost all parts of the town was a view of the surrounding hills dotted with contentedly grazing cattle. Louise enjoyed her weekly excursion to the town. It was a chance to get away and, sometimes, to think. Or occasionally she let her mind go blank allowing her thoughts to wander, to concentrate on nothing.

After leaving the market Louise wandered through Yeovil's main and prestigious store, Denners, with its floors of fashions, furniture and electrical goods. She was not fashion conscious and her daily dress was largely trousers and a top of some description—T-shirt in summer, jersey in winter—sturdy shoes or, occasionally, boots. Wellingtons in wet weather.

Two or three times a year she had her hair cut in Denners' hairdressing salon, but seldom had it set. It had a springy texture and a natural wave and she preferred to wash it herself at home and dry it in front of the fire.

Louise had another cup of coffee in Denners' restaurant and being tempted by nothing in the store she went round the corner to Yeovil's impressive public library, up the stairs to the Reference section and began to search for books on surrogacy.

The reference librarian, tactfully concealing her surprise and curiosity, also advised her to try the Internet and showed her how to use it on the library computer.

There were many different kinds of surrogacy but, basically, a woman carried a child in her womb for another couple either by having her own egg fertilised by the semen of the father of the baby—known as traditional—or having the couple's own embyro implanted in her womb. In this case the surrogate was not the biological mother but a host and had no natural claims at all to the child.

The situation was a minefield of disaster but, nevertheless, there were a number of agencies offering advice, and clinics the means to carry out the whole procedure.

Louise stayed in the library until lunch time surfing the site. Then she shut down the computer, thanked the staff for their help and made her way to the café in The Quedam where she joined the self-service queue for lunch.

She opted for a jacket potato filled with baked beans and a cappuccino and was standing round looking for a seat when she heard herself hailed and espied a hand waving above the heads of the crowd from the back of the restaurant.

'Hi, Louise!' a familiar voice called and she saw her friend Dorothy sitting at a table with her two small children. Dorothy and Louise had been at school together where they were best friends. Neither had been particularly distinguished academically. Dorothy left after 'O' Levels, but Louise stayed on and did 'A' Levels. Dorothy remained in the country and became an assistant at a busy veterinary practice. Louise went up to London and took a secretarial course. They lost touch.

When Louise returned to look after her mother she found that Dorothy had married a vet and was living nearby. She had two children, Andrew and Heather, now aged four and two respectively. The friendship was renewed and strengthened. They began to see each other regularly, and became confidantes again.

'Room for me?' Louise set her tray down on the table.

'Of course, that's why I called you.' Dorothy indicated the seat opposite and Louise sat down and gazed across at her friend.

'What a nice surprise.' She smiled at the children busily digging into their ice creams. 'Isn't Andrew at school?'

'He only goes in the mornings. I had to go and see the doctor today so I took them with me. Sean is very busy with this BSE business.'

'Yes, it's terrible.' Louise dug her fork into her beans, squashing them into her potato to form a gooey mess. After a few mouthfuls she looked enquiringly at Dorothy who was wiping the children's mouths. 'Nothing wrong I hope? I mean, the doctor.'

Dorothy completed her task and grimaced.

'It depends what you mean by "wrong". I'm pregnant.'

'Oh!' Louise was nonplussed. Dorothy's tone was so dead. 'I gather you're not too pleased?'

'It will be the last one,' Dorothy said firmly. 'Sean will have to have the snip or I'll be sterilised after the baby is born.'

'Isn't that a bit drastic?'

'It's drastic but that's what's needed. I don't want any more children. Two is quite enough. Three plenty. Sean is out all hours of the day and night and at weekends. It can be very hard bringing up children virtually on your own.' She sounded aggrieved. Dorothy already had the rather set

25

expression of the dissatisfied wife and, though she never said anything, Louise had for some time had the feeling that the marriage wasn't all it should be.

'I bet.' Louise finished her meal, sat back and stirred her coffee.

'What do you think of surrogates?' Louise asked, abruptly changing the subject. 'Women having babies for infertile couples.'

'Oh, you saw the programme?' Dorothy grimaced. 'I think they're bonkers. There's something really kinky about it if you ask me.'

'Why kinky?'

'What normal woman would want to have a child for someone else?'

'Yes, I suppose you're right.' Louise looked thoughtful.

'Having your own baby is bad enough . . .' Dorothy looked enquiringly at her friend. 'You're on your day out with Buddy?'

'Yes.' Louise glanced at her watch. 'I think I'll stroll back and see if he needs any help.'

'You must bring Buddy round for dinner,' Dorothy patted her stomach, 'before I get too fat and lazy.'

'That would be nice.'

'Shall we look up a day?' Dorothy fished in her hand-bag for her diary and started flicking over the pages. 'The trouble is at the moment I don't know when Sean's free. Look, I'll ring you.'

Louise shrugged on her anorak.

'Anything with Buddy . . . ?' Dorothy put her head on one side. 'You know . . . marriage in the offing?'

'Don't be silly,' Louise vigorously shook her head, 'nothing like that.'

'Louise,' Dorothy leaned towards her and lowered her voice. 'You haven't still got a "thing" about Steve?'

'I haven't got a "thing" about Steve,' Louise retorted irritably.

'But Louise . . .' Dorothy sat back clasping the hand of Heather who had begun to wriggle.

'I want to wee,' Heather said with a note of urgency in her voice.

'I don't really want to talk about it,' Louise got up.

'But I worry about you.' Dorothy also rose still clutching her daughter's hand.

'Well don't, please.' Louise fastened her coat wishing she'd never, in an unguarded moment, confided in Dorothy her feelings about Steve.

'He has never given you the slightest encouragement.'

'How do you know?'

'Well, has he?'

'In many ways, yes. I shan't push him. I shall just wait, but one day . . . I'm sure it will happen. Meanwhile I'm just happy to be near him.'

'Buddy is such a nice guy,' Dorothy said, fastening the children's coats. 'And he loves you. I'm sure he does. You could have such a good life together. How I wish you could fall for him. Sometimes I think you ought to seek help.'

'What do you mean "seek help"?' Louise asked, affronted by Dorothy's tone.

'You know, see a psychiatrist.'

'What rubbish.' She gazed down at Heather. 'You'd better take that child to the loo before she has an accident.'

Dorothy, however, persisted. 'But it isn't normal.

27

Loving a man who gives you nothing, *can* give you nothing . . .'

Louise didn't listen to any more but walked out of the restaurant without saying goodbye.

Friendship was such a fragile thing.

*   *   *

Buddy had had a good day at the market and his stall was practically clear when Louise joined him.

'Ready to pack up?' she asked.

'Do you fancy a film and a meal?' Buddy looked hopefully at her.

Louise shook her head.

'I feel I ought to go back and see how Tina is and if Steve needs any help.'

'Can't you get Steve out of your mind for once?' The despair showed in Buddy's voice.

'If you're going to be silly I shall stop coming with you to market.' Louise turned towards the van. 'In fact I'll stop seeing you altogether.'

*   *   *

Louise knew that she'd gone too far with Buddy. They drove back virtually in silence and he dropped her off at the gates of the manor with only a cursory farewell and without offering to drive her to the door.

'See you,' he'd said and drove off before she had time to reply. She stood for a few moments watching the van disappear round the bend in the road and then walked slowly up the drive. It had not been a very good day. Maybe she should rely less on Buddy. In a way she used him to do all the little jobs that, of course, Steve couldn't do, probably wouldn't do even if he was able.

Buddy was a very good handyman, useful for putting up shelves or digging the garden. He was able to mend the car, the fridge, the washing machine, disperse wasps' nests, unblock chimneys, put his hand to anything that went wrong. He had once painted the house inside and out. He would come round at a moment's notice if she needed him. He was utterly reliable and dependable, untemperamental, calm in an emergency.

His only reward for all this fidelity was an easy camaraderie, but it wasn't what he wanted. Gradually he had revealed his feelings for Louise and she had had to tell him she loved another man. It was even longer before she had confessed that the man was Steve.

Buddy took it well at first. He thought it was a joke, a girlish crush. But when he realised that she was serious, that Steve came between him and the object of his desire, he changed and his attitude kept on swinging between supplication and hostility, which usually expressed itself as derision. Maybe after today he'd get sick of it too. Then she would miss him.

Louise was sorry that she hadn't accepted the invitation to a meal and the cinema. Too late now.

When she got to the manor it was after seven. She went in through the back door and found the kitchen tidy but with a strangely deserted air. Usually there was some evidence of food on the go, someone having eaten or about to eat.

But there was no sign of Mrs Barton or the children. She went into the house via the kitchen corridor off which were rooms that in grander days

29

would have been the cook's parlour and the butler's pantry.

Those days were long past. Steve had no live-in staff, just Mrs Barton and a couple of cleaners. It was a big house to keep clean. In London he had a flat in The Albany. Louise had never been there but she heard it was very nice and spacious.

In a way Steve was a very unassuming man considering the size of his fortune. He was not pretentious. He was obviously ambitious and clever, but he didn't show off or display his wealth, somewhat perhaps to Tina's disappointment.

Like the kitchen the house too was strangely quiet. Louise listened again for the sound of the children's voices but heard nothing. Then she heard a door closing upstairs and a moment later Steve appeared at the head of the grand circular staircase and stopped when he saw her.

'Louise,' he called, running down to join her. 'I thought it was your day off? Isn't it market day?'

Louise nodded. 'I wondered how Tina was. I thought you might need help with the children.'

'That's very kind of you.' He touched her arm gratefully. 'I don't know what we'd do without you. Tina still isn't well. I decided to take the children up to stay with their mother for a few days. Come and have a drink.'

He led the way into the drawing room and to a table on which there was an assortment of bottles.

'Sherry?'

'Whisky might be nice.'

'I forgot you were a whisky woman. I have a very nice Malt.'

'Sounds good.' Louise moved over to the French windows and stood looking out onto the lawn, the herbaceous borders on either side of the lake which were full of spring flowers. Now she was glad she hadn't gone with Buddy. As always she felt the strange, light-headed sense of euphoria whenever she was alone with Steve, the bonus that they might possibly have supper together.

'Did you have a nice day?' Steve asked, joining her and handing her a glass.

'It was alright. Thanks,' she turned and took the glass from him.

'It sounds as though it wasn't so good,' he said. 'I had a day like that too. I decided this morning that Tina needed complete rest. I rang up Frances and she was quite agreeable to having the children. I called the school and cancelled a trip to Germany and up to London we went. Mrs Barton stayed with Tina, gave her lunch. Look,' he glanced at his watch, 'it's nearly eight. Have you eaten?'

'No.'

'Maybe one of your steaks in the kitchen? I'll get a nice bottle of Burgundy from the cellar.'

'Won't Tina eat?' Louise looked anxious.

Steve frowned. 'She said she wasn't hungry. I really feel very worried about her. The doctor thinks the root cause of her trouble is depression. He's put her on an anti-depressant.'

They finished their drinks and walked slowly along to the kitchen. While Steve went down to the cellar to fetch the wine Louise looked in the fridge in the large stone larder for something to eat. There were no steaks but the remains of a cold chicken and to this she added lettuce and tomatoes and was slicing the bread when Steve reappeared, carefully carrying a bottle of wine in a basket as though it was a baby.

'No steak I'm afraid,' she said. 'Cold chicken and salad.'

'We could have eaten out but I don't want to leave Tina.'

'Of course not.' Louise kept her eyes on her task. 'I'll make her a sandwich.'

'But she said . . .' Pursing his mouth Steve began to extract the cork from the bottle. 'She said she didn't want anything to eat.'

'I'll make it nice and tasty. Maybe it will tempt her.'

Louise finished slicing the bread and put the loaf in the breadbin.

'You're amazing,' Steve said admiringly, looking at the well-stocked table nicely set with cutlery, glasses and folded napkins. 'A meal produced in five minutes flat. I don't know what we'd do without you.'

'You keep on saying that. I wish you wouldn't.' Gritting her teeth Louise vigorously applied the carving knife to the chicken.

'But it's true.' Steve poured the wine, tasted it, grunted his approval and began to pour. 'It's a bit cold, but it will soon warm up.' Then he sat down opposite her. 'You're so capable I can't think why you're not married. What about Buddy?' He leaned across the table and helped himself to a slice of bread. 'Why didn't you have a nice day? You always go with him to the market don't you?'

Louise set slices of chicken neatly onto a plate and passed it over to him. The exhilaration she'd felt at the prospect of dinner alone with Steve had begun to evaporate. She was so capable, so efficient. Just like a chum. This was Steve's idea of her. She knew it, but she always hoped it would

32

change.

'I'm not in love with Buddy,' she said finally, sitting down. 'It's as simple as that.'

'Sometimes love comes later.' Steve helped himself to salad, sipped the wine again and pronounced himself more satisfied. 'The bouquet is rising. I thought it would.' He set the glass down again as if enthusing to his task of promoting the virtues of Buddy. 'No, really, sometimes love does come later, so they say. I was in love with both my wives. Still am . . . with Tina that is,' he added hastily.

'Well, there you are. Why do you say love comes later?'

'Because I've heard it does. Look at these arranged marriages. They say they work terribly well. It isn't as though you don't know Buddy. I think he is a very nice chap, and I'm sure he has a shine for you.'

'Can we change the subject?' Louise took a gulp of her wine. Then, afraid of offending him, smiled. 'Please.'

'By all means.' Steve, completely at ease in her company, smiled back. 'What to?'

'If it's not an impertinent question, why can't Tina have children?'

'Oh!' Steve wiped his mouth and leaned back in his chair. 'She has something called Asherman's Syndrome which is damage to the lining of the womb. She can't carry a child. Frequent miscarriages.'

'So IVF is no good?'

'No. We've seen any number of gynaecologists. Hopefully these anti-depressants prescribed by the doctor will help her to come to terms with the

33

situation. I can't think what else.'

Louise said slowly, 'There was a programme on surrogacy. Someone to have your baby for you. Did you ever consider that?'

'We thought of surrogacy because Tina's ovaries are OK. One of the doctors who runs a fertility clinic suggested it. But we would have trouble finding a surrogate, even if we liked the idea, which we don't. It would have to be someone we knew, someone we trusted. Above all someone we liked. In other words an impossible order. Who could you find who would do something like that?'

Without waiting for a reply Steve put his knife and fork together and looked at the kitchen clock.

'I'll go and see if Tina is OK and if she'd like a sandwich. Thank you.' As he passed her he put out his hand and tightly pressed her shoulder. 'You're a brick . . .' Guiltily he transferred his hand up to his mouth and smiled apologetically. 'Oh, I know you don't like me saying that, but you are.'

CHAPTER THREE

She supposed it had stuck in her mind ever since she saw the programme, like an obsession: knowing that Tina couldn't have a baby and it was possible that she could carry one for her. If she couldn't have him herself what better way of getting closer to Steve than by bearing his child? It would give them an unbreakable bond. True, it would not be her baby but she would have nurtured it, given it life.

There would of course be a bond with Tina too.

That was the downside, yet she could see herself living with it. But even as the notion took hold in her mind Louise was convinced that the idea was a pipe dream and that Tina would say 'no'.

However, during the days that followed Louise became more and more obsessed with the conviction that she could do something for Steve which would bind him to her for ever.

Steve, who was usually frequently away from home, was about a lot as Tina failed to respond to her medication and spent most of the time on her bed too listless, apparently, to make the effort to get up and dressed. The children remained with their mother. Steve would go up and down to see them, sometimes spending a night in London but no more.

Louise and Duncan were increasingly busy as the season progressed and the number of visitors to the gardens and garden centre increased.

Steve came often to the shop rather as if he were at a loose end. Usually he was such a dynamo, so full of nervous energy that he found it impossible to sit still. He had to be into everything. He now applied this to an area he felt he had neglected: his small business venture at home. He could see scope for development. He, Duncan and Louise frequently went into a huddle discussing plans for enlarging the centre. It was heady stuff. These were among the most exiting days Louise could remember, having Steve around such a lot, seeing him so involved in improving the centre.

Of course he was not a man to sit around with an ailing wife, though doubtless he spent a lot of time with her. Louise could not pretend to herself that he and Tina were not devoted. But in a curious way

35

she was able to compartmentalise her relationship with Steve, and that of Steve and Tina. She was able to switch off and not think about them together. Steve would come buzzing down fairly early in the morning before the doors were open, and Louise and Duncan were always there early too. Steve sometimes came to them before going over the farm with Frank Barton, or he would come to them first and see Frank later. Louise took to getting there earlier and earlier so that she could have time alone with Steve before Duncan appeared.

The three of them wandered round the estate whether in sunshine or drizzle, whatever the morning offered. Steve usually had plans in his hand and some of his suggestions were vetoed by Duncan, usually for good reasons. Sometimes Louise intervened, but she didn't want to say too much, to appear too opinionated, too knowing. Anyway, Steve had so many good ideas it wasn't necessary. Almost all she had to do was agree.

But they all did manage to agree that there would be a water feature and an emphasis on water plants. There might even be a playground for children, a study centre for students. More and more Steve seemed to warm to the possibilities of what could be made from the facilities at Poynton, and Louise, seeing more of the man she loved than she had for years, basked in the sunshine of his approval, his praise, his obvious appreciation of the effort she was making, particularly with regard to the shop, as Tina interested herself in it less and less.

'We need more stock,' Louise told Steve one day as they checked the inventory together. It was

36

pouring outside and Duncan was working in the greenhouses. It was a gloomy morning and the lights were on in the shop as she and Steve made a tour, inventory to hand.

'These expensive dinner services are hard to move. They're lovely, but Tina thought this too. Tina has very good judgment,' Louise said diplomatically and, pausing, looked sympathetically at Steve. 'How *is* Tina? We see so little of her.'

'A little better. I'm thinking of giving her a complete change and taking her on a cruise. You would be alright, wouldn't you, coping on your own? Would you like an assistant, someone to help you?'

Louise froze. The chill went right through her body. 'How long would you be away?'

'Six months or so. Round the world I think. Tina can relax and maybe this baby problem will stop preoccupying her so much.'

Six months. Six *months* without Steve! Louise momentarily shut her eyes. It couldn't happen. It must not happen. Suddenly an enormous chasm seemed to open at her feet.

Steve turned away from her, examining the stock on the various stands and lining the shelves in the stock-room. The monogrammed beakers, plates and ashtrays. The silver napkin rings, porcelain vases and decorative dishes. The table mats and coasters with pictures of the manor house. The embroidered Irish linen tablecloths and napkins, the fancy tea-towels.

There were boxes of soap, talcum powder and creams. Jars of jam, honey and marmalade. Tins of shortbread and hand-made chocolates. Pots of pickles, red cabbage, onions and assorted spices.

Then there were the plants, some boxed or standing in monogrammed pots. The garden implements, packets of seeds.

There was no end to the temptations offered to the would-be purchaser.

What chances, what opportunities the place offered. Steve felt he had never properly looked into this aspect of the business before, considering it rather as a hobby, something for Tina to do.

'How do we go about replacing the stock? Adding to it?'

'There seems a lot more we could do. There's a huge warehouse near Plymouth. There's also a big garden centre where we can get new ideas. Much of the stuff we have made but much more we buy in.'

'Let's go,' Steve said decisively. 'Would tomorrow be OK? I'll see if Tina feels up to coming. I know she likes to be part of what's going on. I don't want her to feel left out.'

*   *   *

Steve called for Louise just after eight the next morning, knocked on the door and she asked him in. The rain had cleared and the day was fine. Morgan went across to meet him, rubbing himself against Steve's leg.

'You've got this place looking very nice now,' Steve looked round approvingly. 'You did it up since your mother died?'

This showed how long it was since he'd been here—almost two years. 'Buddy decorated it for me inside and out.'

'Good man Buddy,' Steve smiled approvingly.

Louise put on her jacket and looked towards the

door. 'Is Tina with you?'

'No. She said she'd give it a miss. Feels a bit tired. Mrs Barton will keep on eye on her. Shall we get going?'

Louise ushered him through the door, locked up and jumped into the passenger seat of the Range Rover. As he started the engine she gazed ahead, cheeks pink, eyes shining with excitement.

A whole day with Steve. This was almost unparalleled.

During the trip he was very talkative. He told her about his work, projects which he'd had to shelve for the time being, the phasing out of international contacts.

'I've made all the money I shall ever need,' he said. 'I have good managers, so my business virtually runs itself. I love it here and I really would like to expand what we've got at Poynton without spoiling the character of the place. I mean, we don't want to offend anyone in the village. It must be done tactfully and well. They must all approve.'

'Oh but I think no one can possibly object to the water feature. They're becoming so popular. The children's centre can be discreet, away from the village so that there's not too much noise.' Louise paused, frowning. 'Where would you have the study centre, and studying what for instance?'

'Duncan's considering ideas for that. I told him I'd like to develop the arboretum. Maybe we could concentrate on trees?'

'Lovely idea.' Louise hugged her knees. She felt so happy.

*   *   *

39

The large sprawling warehouse on the outskirts of Plymouth supplied goods for stately homes, which were open to the public, and garden centres all over the country with everything from pixies and ornamental furniture to Shetland sweaters. It was quite new to Steve who had left the original stocking of the shop to Louise, and then, after their marriage, Tina, who had been there quite often.

Louise explained how many of the items were ordered here, but those that had to be specially monogrammed or engraved were sent elsewhere and, of course, the very expensive items that were slow movers usually came from London but often from abroad. No stately home and garden centre wanted to look the same as the others, and although there was inevitably repetition, individuality was also of considerable importance.

But in order to be unique Tina had gone to Sèvres and Limoges to order the tea-sets and dinner services, stopping en route in Paris where she bought a lot of personal items for herself including couture clothes. She had never taken Louise on these trips.

Louise felt that Tina obviously kept a lot of things from her husband who displayed an ignorance about the business that quite surprised her.

To him it had been small beer, not very important, but now his interest seemed immense and as they walked round the vast warehouse he asked an enormous number of questions until she was almost exhausted. She was also surprised by the instinctive knowledge he seemed to have about what would do well and what would remain on the shelves until reduced in the sales.

When their order book was almost full, Steve finally looked at his watch.

'Why don't we have some lunch? You must be starving.'

'There's a snack bar here.'

'I think we can do better than a snack bar. If we hurry we're sure to find a pub.'

'There's a very good hotel just down the road. I think they serve until three.'

They hurried out, climbed into the Range Rover and drove the few hundred yards to the hotel which stood in extensive grounds just off the main thoroughfare.

They were greeted with warmth and civility, as befits a first class hotel, and were told that, although the dining room was on the point of closing, of course they would be accommodated. Steve thanked the official as they were ushered into a large, pleasant room in which there were still people eating lunch.

'What a nice place,' Steve said, looking round. 'Have you been here before?'

'No, I usually eat at the snack bar. I've heard it's good.' Louise studied the menu before realising that she was not at all hungry. 'Just an omelette for me.'

'You're sure?' Steve looked up, surprised, then down again at the menu. 'I think I'll have a mixed grill and a pint of lager.'

The waiter took their order; butter and rolls were laid before them. Steve's lager soon arrived and a glass of wine for Louise.

'We've done a good day's work, Louise. I didn't realise it was so extensive. We've come a long way from the shack next to the greenhouses.'

41

'Thanks to you.' Louise suddenly felt humble. It was really Steve with his generosity, his faith in her judgment who had made it all possible. After all, he had rescued her from a humdrum secretarial job and the inevitable but necessary tedium of looking after an ailing mother whom, nevertheless, she had adored. He had given her a new life and subsequent responsibility, trusted her, encouraged her, even spoilt her. He had no doubt of her competence or integrity.

'No, thanks to *you* . . .' Steve insisted, adding as an afterthought, 'and Tina, of course. She picked it up very quickly.'

'She did.' Louise was anxious to appear loyal.

'She was going to be a fashion buyer after giving up modelling. One of the couture houses had offered her a job.' Steve gave a deprecating smile. 'And then she met me.' He frowned. 'You know, Tina has changed. She is not the woman she used to be. I really am quite concerned about her. All her sparkle has left her.'

'It must be very worrying for you.' Louise sipped her wine and wondered how to change the subject. Talking about Tina made her feel uncomfortable: jealous, resentful and disloyal all at the same time. And then there was that germ of an idea hovering at the back of her mind . . . but how to put it? How?

Their food soon arrived and further conversation for the time being became monosyllabic. Finally, his plate cleared, Steve sat back and pronounced himself satisfied with the food.

'How was yours?'

'Excellent.'

'Would you like a sweet?'

'No thanks.'

'Coffee?'

'Please.'

'Let's go and have it in the lounge. I can smoke.'

They moved across the by now deserted dining room into a pleasant lounge where a scattering of people sat, also drinking coffee. Steve drew two chairs close to the huge picture window with a commanding view of the countryside and, taking a small cheroot from a packet in his breast pocket, lit up. He tossed the match into an ashtray and, with a loud sigh of satisfaction, blew a stream of smoke in the air.

'This is nice. A successful day I think.'

'Very.'

'We must go up to London. I realise there is an awful lot about this business I don't know. I think we could do better, expand. What do you think about building a hotel?'

'In the grounds?' Louise looked startled.

'There's plenty of land. It shouldn't be too hard to get planning permission. It would bring jobs and tourists to the area, much needed revenue. We could build on the site of Duncan's cottage. I think that would make planning permission easier to get.'

'What would Duncan say?'

'I don't think Duncan would mind if we offered him something else, a house or cottage in the village. Do you?'

Louise screwed up her nose. 'I don't know that I like the idea of a hotel. I think it's nice and cosy as it is.'

'It is cosy, but it would be a lot more profitable. It could be a really *nice* hotel, like this, a stylish country house hotel. I suppose this was once a gracious home.'

'I suppose it was.' Louise studied the high ceiling with its ornate plasterwork.

'What about turning the manor into a hotel?' Steve paused, as if suddenly struck. 'Say, that *is* an idea.'

'And then what would happen to you?'

'We'd turn the cottage into a house. It would be large enough.'

'Would Tina like that?'

'I'd have to ask her.' Steve thoughtfully drew on his cheroot. 'No, perhaps she wouldn't.' He sighed deeply. 'Anyway, the whole thing is probably a bit far-fetched. I said it on the spur of the moment. Besides, I can't spring too many surprises on Tina. She's not in a fit state . . . Oh, and there is the cruise. I'd forgotten about that. I promised her a cruise. I can't offer upheaval instead, and the building work would take months, if not years, by the time we've dealt with the acres of bureaucracy. Maybe we should postpone the cruise until then?'

Their coffee arrived and Louise poured. She passed Steve his cup, looking at him surreptitiously, wondering if this was the moment. Despite his concerns Steve seemed in a mellow mood, receptive. The lounge was almost deserted with just a couple of businessmen going over plans in a far corner. Steve puffed away at his small cigar and drank his coffee.

There might never be a moment, alone, like this, for some time, if ever.

'Steve,' Louise moved to the edge of her seat. 'I wanted to say something to you and I don't want you to talk until I've finished.'

She began to feel very nervous, her heart jumping about in her chest, her throat very dry.

The change in her manner puzzled Steve, then, as if an idea had occurred to him, alarmed him.

'Don't tell me you're thinking of leaving . . .'

'Nothing like that,' Louise hastened to reassure him. 'But it *is* something unusual. However, I do assure you I have given it a lot of thought, but I haven't known where or how to begin. I still don't.' She gazed down at her lap and began lacing and unlacing her fingers. 'It's just that . . . about Tina's unhappiness, the baby, you know.'

'Oh yes, that.' Steve looked worried again.

'Well, it started me thinking. You remember some time ago we mentioned . . . well, surrogacy. It came up. About a woman having a baby for another . . .'

'But I said . . .' Steve's expression changed, but Louise held up her hand.

'You said it didn't appeal to you unless it was someone you knew and liked. Well . . .' she took a deep breath and leaned even closer towards him. 'I thought I could be that person.' She knew that by now her face was very red. She was agitated, perspiring.

Steve seemed to register no emotion at all but sat back smoking his cheroot and gazing at her.

Desperately Louise went on. 'I may have shocked you, spoken out of turn. If so I'm sorry. I hope it won't change things between us, but I had to say it. It may not be possible, but I don't see why I couldn't have a child, carry it that is, for you and Tina. Of course it wouldn't be *my* baby, biologically. It would be yours and hers. I've done quite a lot of reading. The embryo is implanted . . .

45

you know, in the surrogate womb. That's all there is to it.'

Steve finally found his voice.

'But why do you want to do that? Go to all that trouble?'

'Because you've been very good to me. I've got a job and a lifestyle I would never have had otherwise. I've got security for life. Call it a way of saying "thank you".' She attempted a tremulous smile and in the process looked very attractive.

'And you would be prepared to do all that for me? For us? It's an enormously generous way of saying "thank you" for something quite small.'

'It was big for me. If I could do something big for you in return I would.' Louise nodded emphatically several times. 'I have thought and thought about it. That is if I can, if nothing is wrong. But I read that it is possible for women who haven't had children to be surrogates. I'm strong and healthy. Besides, I don't particularly want my own children and I don't think I'll ever have any.'

'Why not?'

Louise shook her head. 'I don't know. It's just the way I feel.'

'I really don't know what to say.' Shaking his head Steve stubbed out the rest of his small cigar. 'I'm almost speechless.'

'Well,' Louise knew she was gabbling as if, somehow, she had to justify herself, 'you know *me*. You like me I think.'

'I do. I like you, very much. You know that.'

'I do know it,' Louise nodded. 'We've always got on. I think we're close to each other . . . and Tina too, of course. That is if she approves. She may not want it. We need never refer to it again, if . . . you know, if she says "no". It will be as though we had never spoken. But I just thought, for your sake and hers, that I could at least offer . . .'

Louise studied his face, unable to fathom the precise nature of the variety of emotions which seemed to rush over it, one after the other: hope, disbelief, shock, incredulity, happiness, perhaps even fear.

Suddenly he leaned towards her and took her hand. Then he drew her closer and kissed her on the cheek momentarily pressing it firmly to his.

'Thank you,' he whispered in her ear. 'Thank you, thank you, thank you.'

*　　　*　　　*

Tina felt she should have made an effort and gone with Steve and Louise. She could have done if she'd tried, but she felt too lethargic. Steve got up so early and she hated early mornings. Now, having bathed she sat swathed in her white towelling robe in front of her mirror and examined herself critically, dispassionately. She was very pale and she'd lost weight. Thin enough already she'd be skeletal if she wasn't careful.

She was nearly thirty-six and she looked older, and yet with a little effort she knew she could lose five years, maybe even seven. She had good bone structure, deeply recessed sapphire-blue eyes, high cheekbones and her complexion, when she took care of it, was flawless. Her skin, now drained and tired-looking, could be milky white. She was tall— five feet nine—and had had a successful career on the catwalk, not among the mega-salaried models, but certainly in the big league.

Tina had been the product of a broken home, sent off to boarding school at an early age, and insecurity had been part of her life ever since she could remember. Holidays with Mother or Father, never together, and the feeling that neither really wanted her. Seeing her was merely a duty undertaken reluctantly. There never seemed to be much money around, or not enough for school trips or little extras. Or maybe it was that her parents simply didn't want to spend it on her. Her Swedish father had been a wholesale fruit importer.

Thus the threat of poverty and insecurity was very real for her and she had determined to exploit her acknowledged good looks to avoid both these evils.

She went to London when she was seventeen and quickly got work with a model agency. When she was twenty-three she had married Denis Walker who was a merchant banker many years her senior. It was not a love match for her, though Denis was not unattractive.

She had already been a model for five years and she thought this would give her security. There was always the fear among beautiful women with successful careers that one day everything would go: looks, career and that would be that. It was particularly so in the case of Tina, haunted by her background. Denis, already twice married, had teenage twins who were very spoilt and rudely ignored their stepmother whenever they came to visit or stay. Besides that, Tina soon discovered that Denis's hobby, apart from his work, was women. He collected them and, as another celebrated businessman had once said, 'If you marry your mistress you have to replace her,' or

48

words to that effect.

The twins were only too pleased to confirm her suspicions and after less than two years the marriage was over. Important as money was to her, Denis had come to revolt her and any more time spent with him was unthinkable. Because she left him and couldn't actually prove adultery, Tina settled for a quickie divorce and consequently a tiny divorce settlement.

Once more it seemed that poverty beckoned and she resumed her career with less success than before; a lot of photographic work and small-time modelling jobs: catalogues and stores, ready-made instead of couture.

Steve had been a friend, or rather a business acquaintance, of Denis's who had financed some of his ventures. Steve and Frances and Denis and Tina had gone out together a few times before they divorced their respective partners.

They met again at a charity show at the Savoy and Steve began dating her. She fell in love with Poynton and Steve's way of life before she fell in love with Steve and fantasised about being the mistress there, security at last. But Steve was not Denis. He was younger, dynamic and better looking. He seemed to offer her a real chance of a happier and more satisfactory lifestyle and he was as rich, if not richer, than Denis.

She was less than enchanted by the fact that he had two young children in his custody. Her preferment would have been a cosy, if rather capacious nest, and a family of their own with dogs and horses, and the style and all the appurtenances of a well-heeled country life that one read about in magazines. She had no qualms about abandoning the chance of a new career on the business side of a couture house to become Mrs Lockwood.

Tina had always wanted a family to make up for the one she never had, but Denis hadn't. He was nearly fifty when they married and was firm about having no more children. What clinched the matter was that Tina knew the hateful twins would be horrible to any new sibling.

Eventually Tina had the man, she had the house but the babies didn't come. Several times she missed a period and thought she might be pregnant and each time she miscarried, very early on at about three months.

She was advised to keep occupied and busied herself in the shop. They consulted specialists, fertility experts and it was finally discovered that the lining of her womb was too damaged to carry a child. It would never happen.

She had never been so keen on motherhood than when she realised it would be an impossibility and this was when the depression set in and the setbacks and ill health started. Tina tried to concentrate on the shop, but she started having headaches, and now she was on anti-depressants and permanently fatigued.

Patient as he was, she knew that if she carried on like this she would lose Steve, and the truth was that she had really fallen in love with him.

Tina finished examining her face and then started vigorously to massage it, cleansing it, toning, applying soft creams and rubbing them in well to soften that dry taut skin. Finally, carefully and painstakingly she began to make herself up as she used to in the days on the catwalk. She was an expert and knew how to make herself look good.

She would give Steve a nice surprise when he came home. So, after the make-up she dressed with care in a trouser suit made of swirling black voile she had bought at Courreges during her last trip to Paris. She fastened a gold belt round her slim waist and put on very high-heeled Manola Blahnik sandals.

Then she went downstairs to discuss a menu with Mrs Barton. She wanted something special that night for Steve, as though they were marking a new beginning.

*   *   *

'Did you have a good day?'

Smiling, Tina came over to Steve and placed a glass of whisky in his hand. He looked up gratefully, pleased and also astonished by the sudden change not only in her appearance but her entire demeanour and took the glass from her.

'Excellent. We bought a lot of stock.' He tasted his drink and patted the place beside him on the sofa. As she sat down his arm encircled her waist. 'I'd no idea there was so much to do.'

'I wish I'd come with you,' Tina sipped her own drink.

'So do I.' Steve paused and gazed at her. 'You look lovely,' he said kissing her cheek. 'Do you feel better, darling?'

'Much, much better.' Tina clung to him for a few minutes then drew away, touching her hair. 'I've been feeling really rotten, but now I think I'm on the mend.'

'That's wonderful news, darling.'

'We can plan our holiday. Do you really mean

51

for six whole months?'

Steve frowned and removed an imaginary fly from his drink.

'Maybe not just yet. I've a lot of plans. Look,' he swallowed his drink and consulted his watch. 'I'm starving. I'll tell you about them after dinner.'

There were candles on the dining-room table, the best plate and silver, the lights turned low. Tina and Mrs Barton between them had gone to some trouble to arrange the setting for a perfect evening.

There was a simple meal of very thinly sliced smoked salmon with lemon and brown bread, chateaubriand with salad and a fine Clos de Vougeot to drink, and summer pudding.

The conversation was desultory during the meal, but each was aware of an atmosphere of delicious tension, almost like the dawn of renewed intimacy.

Steve told Tina more about the day, his surprise at the extent of the warehouse, his ignorance, an ignorance he said he intended to do something about.

'I really do want to become more interested in affairs here.' Steve gazed ruefully at the remains of the marvellous wine. 'I want to spend time with you . . . and other things.' His voice trailed off.

'Is that why we're suspending the holiday?' Tina's tone was crisper, sharper, as if she was trying to control her disappointment.

'Not "suspending", "postponing" but not for long. I have a lot to discuss with you. Shall we have a cognac?' He put out a hand and they strolled into the drawing room where a fire had been lit and roared up the chimney.

'Chilly,' Steve said, rubbing his hands together, partly from nervousness as well as the cold, while

Tina poured the drinks. 'You'd never think it was August. Thank you darling.'

He accepted the drink and kissed her again, this time firmly on the lips. 'I can't tell you how incredibly beautiful you look tonight, really sexy and desirable.'

Their lips met again and this time their bodies moulded together, remaining so for a long time.

'Shall we go to bed?' Steve murmured eventually in her ear, 'and forget coffee?'

*   *   *

It was a glorious session of lovemaking, one of the best they had had, and there had been many. After what seemed like hours they lay together, Tina resting in his arms, their legs still entwined, the brandies untouched by the side of the bed.

'I wish . . .' Tina began then stopped. 'Well you know what I wish . . .'

Steve gently disengaged himself and leaned over to look at the time, his mind not yet made up. He knew what she wished. Somehow there was always the same air of tenderness and regret after they made love: fulfilment yet not fulfilment.

Tina sat up and Steve put his arm round her again and hugged her.

'I don't quite know how to put this,' he began, 'and I want you to hear me out.'

'What is it?' Always tense and nervous, beset by real or imaginary fears lurking in the background, suddenly she looked afraid.

'Nothing to worry about,' he squeezed her reassuringly. 'On the contrary. If you agree, it may be possible for us to have a baby . . .'

'*Agree*?' Astonished, Tina gazed at him.

'Louise has offered to be a surrogate . . .'

'*Louise*!' Tina's voice was sharp, indignant. 'What do you mean "Louise has offered to be a surrogate"? Did you *ask* her?'

'Of course I didn't. The idea would never have occurred to me. But Louise knows how much you want a baby . . . we want one. You told her. Well, she has been thinking about it for a long time and read about it and now she has offered.'

'So this is how you spent the day with Louise? Discussing babies. Strange, I must say.'

'No, not at all.' Steve suddenly became defensive. 'We spent the day going round the warehouse.'

'Then how on earth did a subject like this come up?'

Steve turned to her placatingly. 'Now hang on, don't get excited and don't be cross . . . After the warehouse visit, where we worked hard, we had lunch and we were talking and Louise began rather in the way that I did to you just now. She said she didn't know how to put it.'

'I've never *heard* anything so bizarre,' Tina said angrily.

'But why?' Nonplussed, Steve gazed at her. 'Just what is so bizarre?'

'Louise . . .' she began and then stopped as if not knowing how to proceed.

'But, Tina, you *like* Louise. She likes you. She's a friend of the family. A good friend. That's the whole point.'

'But why should she do such a thing? What is her motive? Think of all the trouble. Surely no one would go through such a procedure for nothing? I wouldn't. Is it money?'

'Not at all. Money was never mentioned, though we'd pay all expenses, naturally. She hasn't got a particular motive. She just wants to be helpful. Frankly I think she's a brick even to consider it.' Now it was Steve's turn to feel angry. 'After all, Tina, we discussed surrogacy before and said if it was to happen it had to be someone we knew and liked. That made the whole thing seem impossible.'

'That was a long time ago. I never thought Louise . . . What is her motive do you suppose?'

'She has no motive for God's sake. Why should she have a "motive"? She's trying to be helpful, and very very kind.'

Tina sank back against the pillow. 'She's after something. She's after you. I've always vaguely suspected she fancied you, and the whole thing is a plan to get you.'

'Oh, that is rubbish.' Steve withdrew his arm, angry at the disastrous aftermath of such glorious lovemaking. 'I have known Louise for years. We are just good friends.'

'That's what you think, but I have my doubts. I see how she looks at you. This is just a way to get you. It's sick, if you ask me.'

Steve swung his legs over the side of the bed and sat rubbing his chin wearily. This had not been the time, the place or the moment. He'd handled it badly, muffed the whole thing. 'I'm very sorry I said anything. Forget it.'

He got up and went into the bathroom where he furiously showered, resentful at the way Tina had misconstrued everything.

When he came back to bed Tina had her eyes tightly shut and he put out the light without

55

speaking. She turned her back on him and he sensed she was sobbing.

'I'm sorry,' he said, gently touching her shoulder. 'It would be *our* baby you know, not hers. There would be no sex or anything like that. It would all be done in the laboratory. It's clinical, but it will still be our child, loved and wanted the more so because of all we would have done to get it. As for Louise, she's doing it for the most altruistic of motives. I'm certain of that.'

CHAPTER FOUR

Louise wished now that she'd never spoken to Steve. His attitude towards her had changed and she thought he was avoiding her. After the heady euphoria of their day out together he seemed cold and remote.

Tina's attitude too was different. She appeared anxious to avoid being alone with her in the shop, trotting off to see Duncan or going back to the house whenever there was a lull.

The weather was poor. Poynton was well off the beaten track so people had to make a deliberate detour to find it. It was not the sort of place well signposted but sat cosily, almost mysteriously, in a valley off the main road between Yeovil and Honiton. Few people wanted to visit a garden centre and consume Dorset cream teas when it was pouring with rain.

Louise was alone in the shop. It had again been very wet and, consequently, a slack afternoon. She hadn't seen Tina all day. She busied herself unpacking the goods that she and Steve had chosen from the warehouse and which had just been delivered. She supposed she'd have to wait for Tina's decision as to where they should go.

Entering the shop from the stock-room she saw Steve talking to Duncan. He had a large plan in his hand and she wondered if he was already telling him about his ideas for his cottage. Duncan was a bachelor and Louise felt sure he would be amenable; but would he like the idea of a hotel? Somehow she didn't think so.

Louise returned to the stock-room, inventory in hand, and busied herself until it was time to close. When she returned to the shop Steve was standing by the till cashing up, something very rare for him.

'A poor day,' he said, looking up.

'I'm afraid you have to expect this with the weather.' Louise tried to sound non-committal.

'I've had a chat with Duncan,' Steve closed the till and leaned against the counter. 'He doesn't like the idea of a hotel.'

'Neither do I. Did you . . .' Louise paused, 'did you discuss it with Tina?'

'No. Not yet. But I did tell her . . . you know, what we talked about the other day.'

'I knew she wouldn't be keen,' Louise said defensively.

'It's not that. She's just not ready for it. It will take some time to sink in. Maybe I chose a bad time to tell her.'

'And maybe I shouldn't have said anything.' Louise began to feel embarrassed. How different the atmosphere was now to that day. She wished she'd kept her mouth shut.

Steve frowned.

'Have you regretted it, changed your mind? Didn't you mean it?'

'Oh, no. I meant it. But I think you've been avoiding me, and Tina has too.'

'It was the shock. I felt very awkward facing you. I didn't choose the right moment with Tina.'

'Maybe Tina doesn't like me.'

'Not at all,' Steve said, reassuringly. 'She likes you. We both do, very much. You know that. It's simply that the idea takes some getting used to.'

'I wonder if I should leave?' Louise blurted out. 'I seem to have created an awkward situation.'

'Leave. Leave here?' Now it was Steve's turn to appear shocked. 'Louise, we couldn't do without you. And I don't just mean Tina and myself. I mean the whole place. You're the linchpin.' He put a hand on her arm. 'Please don't think of going. I won't hear of it. You're part of the family, not merely an employee.'

*   *   *

He really cared for her very deeply, Louise told herself as she walked home after closing the shop. The sky had cleared and the sun now smiled on rain-drenched fields. Still high in the sky it bathed the landscape in its mellow light.

It was really a beautiful village. A wonderful part of the world. She was very fortunate to live here, and with Steve to herself it would, should have been perfect.

She thought that one day, perhaps quite soon, he would realise this. In his heart of hearts he probably already did, but wouldn't admit it.

As Louise neared her cottage she saw that

58

Buddy was busy in her garden tidying it up for the autumn. She was about to call out when he disappeared round the side of the cottage with a garden fork in his hand. At the same time a car drew alongside her and, looking up, she saw it was a white Porsche with Tina, hands on the wheel, gazing at her.

'Hi!' Tina said in a markedly friendly fashion. 'Just on your way home?'

'Yes.' Louise approached the car and put a hand on the open window.

'Have you been busy?'

'Not very.' Louise looked up at the sky. 'The weather has been so awful all day.'

'Yes it has.' Tina looked as though she was uncertain about what to say next. Then, 'Do you think I could come in and have a word?' She glanced across to Louise's cottage. 'It's such a pretty cottage isn't it, and do you know I've never been inside?'

'Of course,' Louise pointed ahead and began to lead the way, Tina slowly following her in the car.

The reason Tina had never been inside was that they had never socialised. Theirs was a friendship, if you could call it such despite Steve's reassurances, based solely on the business and, Louise reasoned, maybe there was also a suspicion of jealousy if Tina felt that Steve cared a little too much about her.

As she opened the garden gate Buddy rounded the corner this time carrying his fork laden with manure.

'Hi!' he said looking beyond her. 'Have you got a visitor?'

Tina got out of the car and came slowly towards

59

them. As usual she looked sophisticated and beautiful in a white linen suit, high-heeled white calf shoes. She'd probably been to London.

'Hello Buddy,' Tina said, 'haven't seen you for a long time.'

She gave him a cool, detached smile and Buddy looked at her apologetically. 'Sorry I can't shake hands. I'm manuring the flower beds.'

He crossed in front of them and threw his forkful on the roses.

'How lucky you are to have him,' Tina said as Louise closed the door behind her.

'I'm very lucky. Would you like a drink?'

'That would be marvellous,' Tina agitatedly fanned herself with her hand and sat down. 'I've had such an exhausting day in London.'

'Did you drive?'

'Oh, no. I took the car to the station. I had lunch with Frances, the children's mother. She's really rather nice.'

'Gin and tonic?' Louise uncapped the bottle without looking at her.

'Divine.' She accepted the glass from Louise with a smile. 'I thought Buddy seemed very at home. Are you . . .' she looked enquiringly around, 'that is, do you . . .'

'We don't live together, if that's what you're trying to ask.'

'I see. I thought . . .' Tina sipped her drink. Her agitation was returning. 'Well, I thought . . . you know Steve told me about . . . that you suggested . . .'

Louise sat down, a glass in her hand, and studied the floor.

'Do you still feel the same?' Tina burst out.

Louise nodded without looking at her. 'I

suppose so.'

'Oh!' Tina sounded dejected. 'Have you gone off the idea?'

Louise shook her head.

'I just feel that you've both been rather odd with me in the last couple of weeks, avoiding me.'

'It *was* difficult,' Tina acknowledged. 'I was quite taken aback at first.'

'Steve only told me today how you'd reacted. I quite understand.'

'It's an incredibly . . . well,' Tina fiddled with the jewels on her wedding finger, 'I don't quite know how to say this. It *is* a most generous offer. At first I couldn't understand it. Is it that you want to have a baby . . .' her voice floated away in the air.

Louise vigorously shook her head. 'Not at all. I felt very sorry for you. It must be awful when you can't have something you want so badly.'

'It was a genuine offer then?'

'Oh yes . . . at the time.'

'But now . . . you *have* changed your mind haven't you?' A note of despair entered Tina's voice.

Louise shook her head again. 'No, I haven't changed my mind, but I don't want it to spoil the relationship if, that is, you've changed yours.'

'I'm gradually coming round to the idea,' Tina faltered. 'I wanted to talk to you without Steve. It is *very* strange to think of another woman bearing one's child, and I wasn't sure why you would do it. What your motivation would be. I mean,' she stared at the door, 'would Buddy . . . have you discussed it with him?'

'Not yet,' Louise said cautiously suddenly conscious that Tina was throwing her a lifeline.

'I mean, I *assume* there is an attachment between you?'

'Yes, of a sort,' Louise said offhandedly.

'That's good.' Tina sat back looking as though a weight had been taken off her mind. 'I mean, if we did go ahead and everything went well, Buddy would be a support?'

'I suppose so.'

Tina rose, smoothing her skirt.

'We need to think about it a lot more. Discuss it openly. You have thought of all the consequences? It's not an easy thing and you must know what you're doing. It won't be your baby, not at all. You realise that, don't you?'

Louise also rose and gave a nervous smile. 'If we did go ahead I'd know quite well what I was letting myself in for.'

*   *   *

It was a short cruise rather than the trip round the world Steve had promised, but they had been lucky and the Mediterranean weather had not disappointed. They had joined the boat at Marseilles and it had hugged the coastline of the French and Italian Rivieras as far as Naples where it anchored in the beautiful bay. They embarked on day trips to Pompeii and Herculaneum, staring with some awe at the impressions made by petrified bodies in the volcanic ash two thousand years before.

The boat turned round at Amalfi and, again never far from the coast, made its way back towards Marseilles while the weather continued to be calm despite the nip in the air marking the approach of autumn.

Steve and Tina were due to disembark at Monte Carlo and fly home from Nice. Steve was a restless man who found that relaxing holidays had, in fact, the opposite effect. They made him anxious to keep his finger on the pulse of his many businesses. He was seldom far from his mobile phone or laptop with its essential E-mail and fax facilities.

But still it had been a good time, Tina thought, watching him as he snoozed in the afternoon sun on the prow of the elegant vessel which cut a white swathe through the still blue sea. There had been many romantic dinners either ashore at a quayside trattoria, or in the fine restaurant of the boat which only took 150 passengers whom it smothered in luxury. They had a stateroom on the deck, a steward who appeared at the touch of a button, the services of a valet and a maid should they be required.

That night the boat would anchor in Monte Carlo Bay. They planned to disembark, dine ashore and the next day they would fly home.

Tina sat back and gazed at the sky. She'd just had a dip in the pool and her skin glowed. Momentarily she closed her eyes and when she opened them Steve was gazing at her.

'Sleepy, darling?'

'Pleasantly weary.' Tina passed her hand across her brow and smiled.

'Looking forward to going home?'

'Not as much as you. I think I could do with another week.'

Steve stretched his legs in front of him. 'Oh, I'm enjoying myself, much more than I expected. I mean I love being alone with you, but . . . time hangs heavily when you keep on remembering that there is so much to do.'

'Are you *really* serious about the hotel?'

'More than ever. I've thought about it a lot. I want to expand the whole of the Poynton estate, turn it into a thriving business. It will mean I'll also spend more time at home. I'll cut down on a lot of overseas visits. There'll be more time . . .' he looked at her searchingly, 'if we have a baby . . .' he paused, 'to be together as a family.'

He watched her carefully to see her reaction but Tina's eyes were once again closed as if she was sleeping and perhaps hadn't heard what he'd said.

*　　　*　　　*

Below them the myriad lights of Monte Carlo and the tiny Principality of Monaco against the inky black sky had a fairy tale-like quality. However much one saw the same scene on picture postcards or in films it always seemed to engender a fresh sense of enchantment when seen in reality, with the ghostly reflections of the yachts anchored in the bay, many with their riggings lit up, and the illuminated castle, the ancient home of the Grimaldis, perched on its commanding promontory overlooking the sea as if still ready to repel any invaders.

They had taken a taxi up the steep, winding hill to Beausoleil to a small restaurant which Steve had visited before when he was married to Frances. They had spent most of their honeymoon on the Riviera. The proprietor had changed, so had the decor but the food was just as good.

They had left the boat at noon, booked into a

hotel and Steve immediately rang the restaurant who promised him a terrace table. Tina looked remarkably, almost uncharacteristically relaxed and happy. The purpose of the holiday, at least in Steve's mind, had been achieved. The tension appeared to have left her; the worry lines from her forehead and the dark rings under her eyes had almost disappeared.

They were rather glad now to be off the boat and on their own before the flight from Nice the following day. They sat on the terrace of the restaurant, lingering over their coffee, taking in the gently perfumed night air.

'Would you like to live here?' Steve asked suddenly, taking Tina by surprise.

'Why, are you thinking of it?'

'Not at all. I simply wondered,' he leaned across the table and took her hand. 'I just want you to be happy. You know how much I love you.'

She looked so beautiful with her naturally blonde, almost white gold, hair, those fascinating eyes, the curved, slightly provocative mouth. Her make-up was skilfully applied so as to seem entirely natural and the little worry lines which, inevitably, had aged her, also added to her mystery as though she was a woman who had lived as, indeed, she had. She was a woman of experience, a woman, also, who had suffered on account of her deeply insecure childhood, the break-up of her first marriage.

White was her favourite colour, for winter and summer. She wore a lot of it and now she had on a short white dress, made for evening, simple but also subtly stylish, sleeveless to show her brown arms, and with a low neckline.

Tina saw the expression on Steve's face, the love in his eyes and squeezed his hand. For some reason she felt very close to tears. It had been a wonderful holiday and now that the time had come, she was in a way rather sad to be going home to an English winter when it was still possible in the South of France to eat out of doors at the end of September.

Not only to that, but to problems too. She was rather fearful about the disorganisation the hotel complex would cause. Wouldn't it intrude on their lives? Would the chaos be too awful? That was the debit side. The plus side was that Steve promised to spend more time at home . . . but the subject which she knew was on both their minds she had resolutely refused to discuss every time he came remotely near to mentioning it. Her emotions were mixed—dread on one hand, an almost delicious sense of anticipation on the other.

Steve seemed able to divine what was on her mind. 'I'm perfectly willing to go through with it, if you are. For us it is not so much trauma as for Louise, physically anyway. Emotionally it's colossal.'

Tina's response was measured, careful.

'I *have* been thinking about it,' she said slowly. 'It has never been very far from my thoughts all the time we've been away. I wanted to try and get it sorted out before I spoke to you. Oh, I know you've attempted to bring it up, and you think I have been avoiding it, but I wanted to be clear before I said anything.'

She let go of his hand and leaned across the table.

'I have been thinking about Louise. Louise is the problem.'

66

'But she . . .' Steve began.

Tina held up her hand. 'Give me a chance to speak, please, darling. I was worried about Louise. In many ways she is a mystery. I always think she's holding something back. What concerned me was that I did, and in some ways still do, think she is very attached to you. Oh, alright, you may say it's Platonic and perfectly natural, you've known each other a long time; but sometimes watching her when you're about I think it isn't. There's a certain look in her eyes.'

'I think you're imagining it. I'm sure it's because I knew Louise before I married you. It should reassure you that *you* are the one I love.'

'But how about her? For her to suggest having your baby made me . . .' Tina shuddered as if something had crawled over her flesh. 'And then supposing something went wrong? People die in childbirth. It can be dangerous. But, more importantly, it gives Louise a bond with us that I didn't want, especially living so near. How will she be with the child after it is born? Won't she feel proprietorial?'

Steve shrugged as if he didn't know the answer to that either and he had to remind himself that it was Tina who had wanted the baby, not him, except that he wanted to make her happy. Perhaps it would cause too many problems? Once again he felt assailed by doubt.

Tina placed her long cool hand on his.

'Just before we left I went and saw Louise in her cottage . . .'

'But you didn't say . . .'

'No. I didn't. I wanted to talk to her alone, but it wasn't so much that that was important as the fact

67

that I saw Buddy working in the garden. He seemed perfectly at home. I hadn't realised their relationship was so close.'

'Yes it is close,' Steve said eagerly. 'I'm sure it is, although she is reluctant to admit it. I think Buddy is in love with her and wants to marry her. I don't know why she holds back, and I've told her so. He is such a nice fellow.'

Tina looked relieved.

'So there *is* a relationship?'

'Oh yes,' Steve said reassuringly, 'without a doubt.'

'You mean they're in love? Or is it just him?'

'I think she hesitates but I don't quite know why. If I try and bring it up she always changes the subject. Probably she thinks it is none of my business.'

'They don't live together.'

'That doesn't mean they're not in love.'

'But do you think they sleep together?'

'I suppose so.' Steve shrugged again. 'Does it matter?'

Tina still appeared dissatisfied.

'Isn't it very odd, even perverse, that she should do what she has suggested doing for us if she is in love with another man?'

'I should think it would put your mind at rest. If she is in love with Buddy she is hardly likely to fancy me.'

'And you really don't think Buddy would *mind*? I mean, he might want children and object to the woman he wants to marry doing what is, after all, rather a bizarre thing.'

Steve sat back, thoughtfully sipping the brandy he had ordered with his coffee. Replacing his glass he leaned towards her and spoke urgently.

'If Louise *is* romantically involved with someone else that should ease your mind. Make you feel more relaxed. It is a big thing to take on for all of us. But I think the situation is not nearly as complex as you imagine it to be.'

Tina nodded, a little half-smile playing on her face as though something important had resolved itself. Steve took her hand again, suddenly overwhelmed by a strange and unusual sensation of peace and contentment as if everything would be for the best in the best possible world.

*   *   *

Tina looked very well, her normally pale skin tanned and vibrant, her blonde hair almost honey-coloured. Steve also looked well but was not quite so brown. Over drinks in the drawing room Tina had laughingly explained to Louise how he spent most of the day at sea in their stateroom with his mobile phone and laptop. They were a golden couple Louise thought, not without envy, but she reassured herself with the knowledge that, really, it was all show.

Tina wore a blue trouser suit, fashionably flared trousers, a silk scarf tucked into the neck of her jacket, a large gold brooch on her lapel. No matter what she wore she always looked stunning; her make-up was subtle. She was a practised artist at bringing out her best features.

Louise never wore make-up. She had good skin, good bone structure, bold features, and she had never felt the need for any artificial aid. Her brown eyes were clear because she didn't smoke, hardly drank, walked a lot and usually enjoyed eight hours' sleep every night. Her tawny hair with natural highlights, washed daily, always had a spring, its bouncy curls cut rather close to her head. Tina was tall, but Louise was taller. Tall and strong. She always seemed to exude clean living and good health, the antithesis of Tina with her fragile beauty, a hint of the sick room in the style, perhaps, of the Lady of the Camellias. Louise never dressed up, but for an evening occasion might wear black trousers and a shirt or jersey. Tonight she wore black velvet cords and a black polo neck top because it was cold.

Steve looked just as he always did. He didn't dress up either, but his corn-coloured hair had been bleached by the sun and wind and his keen blue eyes, which never missed a thing, were as always to Louise, mesmerising, amazing.

The first thing Steve had done when he saw her in the shop was to tell her he'd missed her.

Now why had he said that if he didn't mean it?

And how she'd missed him. For Tina the days flew by, for Louise they dragged. Her heart had skipped several beats when she saw him again through the greenhouse glass talking to Duncan over plans laid out on one of the benches.

She had never had dinner with Steve and Tina together. This was a unique, almost solemn, occasion. The purpose was unspecified, but she thought she knew what it was.

If Tina felt nervous she didn't show it. Steve appeared thoughtful, Louise calm.

They talked about the plans for the new complex. Duncan was coming round and so, Louise thought, was she. Apparently it would mean that

Steve would cease most of his travelling. It would be a bigger role for her, apart from which she would be near him all the time. For someone who had never had very much real responsibility, usually worked as a secretary or somebody's assistant it had an added appeal.

There were just the three of them for dinner. Buddy was politely enquired after but he was not invited.

The meal was excellent, prepared for them by Mrs Barton; avocado vinagrette with giant Mexican prawns, rack of lamb and vegetables, apricot tart. There was an Australian Shiraz to drink with the lamb. It was all very good, the atmosphere warm. But Louise preferred the kitchen suppers she and Steve used to share before he married Tina.

The conversation was about trivialities, mainly the trip along the coasts of France and Italy and the plans for the complex. Tension developed, everyone slightly on edge. Louise knew that it was all a preparation for something else: the real purpose of the evening. She felt reasonably in control but when they left the dining room and went back into the drawing room she began to feel distinctly nervous.

Tina wandered over to a table and poured coffee. The percolator bubbling away had been left on a hot plate beside small white porcelain cups, a jug of cream and mint chocolates wrapped in gold foil.

'Brandy?' Steve asked. Louise shook her head.

'I know you're a whisky girl. I've a fine Malt.'

'Nothing thanks.'

'Nothing for me either, darling, thank you,' Tina said sweetly, passing Louise her coffee. Then she sat down opposite her while Steve perched on the arm of her chair, a glass in his hand.

It was a very beautiful room, large with cream-coloured walls and parquet floors. Persian rugs were scattered about, two large sofas faced each other on either side of the magnificent fireplace and there were a few well-placed armchairs, and exquisite antique tables on which several up-market glossy magazines appeared to have been carelessly tossed. No ceiling lights, but plenty of lamps casting deep shadows on the floor.

For a moment there was silence as all eyes were turned to the crackling flames leaping up the chimney.

Finally it was Steve who spoke. 'About what we discussed,' he began, and then, unusually for him, he seemed to lose his nerve and buried his nose in his glass.

'We would like to take up your offer.' Tina carefully edged forward in her chair, ankles neatly crossed, only her tightly clenched hands betraying her nervousness. 'That is if you still feel the same.'

Louise studied the floor; the pace of her heart had quickened; her lips felt dry.

'Of course, *if* you agree there are a lot of things we have to do,' Steve added. 'We have to have thorough medical checks. Consultations with the doctors. We thought it important to have a proper legal agreement. There is the question of expenses. It is full of complexities but there is no reason, with goodwill, why it should not work out . . . if you haven't changed your mind.'

Louise looked up and saw how anxious his expression was. She felt a surge of such tender love for him, such a bond that it was as though they

72

were alone together, that Tina wasn't in the room.

Yes, she would have Steve's baby; but for him not for her. She gazed at Tina whose expression was strange too, not surprisingly.

For would not she, Louise, become the most important person in Steve's life by carrying his child? Wouldn't he have to nourish and cherish her, excluding all others?

CHAPTER FIVE

The clinic was set in acres of parkland and was rather like the exclusive country house hotel Steve was planning to build on the Poynton estate a hundred miles away. The vestibule had concealed lighting, an expanse of expensive carpet, low-slung sofas and chairs, and a fountain playing in the middle, cascading its waters into a large dish filled with exotic fish. An impeccably groomed, uniformed receptionist, sometimes a man but usually an attractive woman, welcomed clients and took details.

What made it unlike Steve's planned hotel was the atmosphere when you got beyond the double doors and saw the white, antiseptic looking corridors gleaming with chrome, the fire extinguishers, the occasional steel trolley laden with medical accoutrements outside a half-open door.

This was serious business involving lots of money and the hopes of infertile couples who came to the world-famous clinic for treatment from far and wide.

Now that at last she was alone and the implantation was about to take place—Steve's sperm having fertilised Tina's egg in the laboratory two days before—Louise had her first real moment of doubt that amounted to a cold sense of fear, almost of detachment, disorientation from her surroundings. That morning the final examinations had been made, tests completed, blood pressure and temperature taken. They all showed that she was a healthy woman of thirty-one, capable of conceiving a child and also of bearing one, even if it was for someone else.

In a way, if ever she did want children, it was reassuring to learn that she should be able to do so without complications.

They had been busy months since that dinner with Steve and Tina the previous September. There had been sessions with the fertility experts, two psychologists, any number of tests, ultrasounds, injections and, latterly, daily tablets of oestrogen to build up the lining of the womb.

Tina and Louise had had to synchronise their cycles so that Louise's womb was ready to receive Tina's egg. The local GP and his practice nurse had been helpful, if a little bewildered and were, of course, sworn to secrecy.

Louise realised she hadn't thought the thing through when the heady idea had come to her, nearly a year before, to tighten her bond with Steve by having his baby. Of course it was Tina's too and this aspect had very much been ignored in her calculation. Yet she had stuck it out with grim determination, never really thinking of crying 'Stop!' until today when Steve and Tina had visited her, knowing that the fertilised egg was in the

74

laboratory waiting to be implanted and grow, hopefully, inside the carefully prepared and receptive womb of Louise. As they went out of the door she had to restrain a feeling of wanting to rush after them and ask to be taken home.

There had been a curious awkwardness, a finality about the meeting. The rapport that they had worked hard to establish in the last five months now seemed non-existent. Tina also looked as though she had doubts, and didn't attempt to kiss Louise when she said goodbye. Only Steve appeared happy and his kiss on her cheek was, by contrast, warm and confident. They were to stay at a nearby hotel and drive Louise home the following day.

The door opened and Janice Carter peered round the door, white-coated, stethoscope around her neck, looking as usual brisk and efficient.

She was a woman of about Louise's age, unmarried and had been both her doctor and counsellor since the first visit to the clinic shortly before Christmas when the detailed examinations began. She had seemed very uncertain at first that Louise was doing the right thing, suspicious of her motives. Now she stood by the side of the bed, hands in her pockets, looking down at her patient as if she still had her doubts.

'It's not too late . . .' she began.

'It is,' Louise said firmly, 'and I have no doubts. None at all. It is just a very difficult time, but I can't let Steve down.'

Janice perched on the side of the bed and took Louise's hand.

'You *are* in love with Steve aren't you?'

'No,' Louise lied, as she had lied in the course of

the many conversations she'd had with Janice and other doctors and counsellors who had emphasised what a big step she was taking, full of complications and rather unusual in a woman who had not had children and whose motivation was clearly not money. What else could it be but some emotional involvement with the natural parents which was not necessarily healthy?

But Louise had learned to conceal her true feelings, and her true motivation. She had become an expert at deception so much so that she was not about to reveal them now.

'We're ready then.' Janice got up. 'Ready when you are.'

'Ready,' Louise said slipping off the bed as Janice opened the door. The theatre orderly came in with a wheelchair, helped Louise into it and, with Janice carrying Louise's file walking behind, trundled her into the theatre a short distance along the corridor where Dr Marsden, the senior gynaecologist and director of the clinic, was waiting for her, masked and gowned.

'Are we ready?' he asked her with a cheery smile.

'Ready,' Louise said and climbed onto the table prepared for the inelegant procedure of hitching her legs through the attached stirrups. In the corner Janice put on her gown and mask, scrubbed her hands in the sink and pulled on her rubber gloves as she took her place by Dr Marsden's side.

Often the natural parents were present at the procedure, as if they were at a birth, but neither Steve nor Tina had requested it, and Louise didn't want it, not with Steve seeing her like this. For her it was too emotional. The birth was another matter. She was going to have to think about that. She looked at Dr Marsden preparing the dish that contained the fertilised egg, while Janice held the pipette that would insert it into her womb.

'It's a beautiful embryo,' Dr Marsden said, scrutinising the gelatinous blob inside the dish. 'Let's hope it works.' Then, as he came towards her, she shut her eyes and tried to imagine that she was with Steve and they were making the baby together and not in this impersonal, clinical way.

* * *

'You're sure you'll be alright?' Tina looked anxiously round the living room of Louise's cottage where a fire had been lit, flowers placed in a large bowl on the table to welcome her home. All Mrs Barton knew was that Louise had to have some small woman's operation, but she was spared the details. Buddy was told nothing at all having by now almost got used to Louise disappearing for days on end. He knew better than to cross-examine her.

Louise looked round too as if she was entering a new and strange domain. There was no reason for everything to look different, but somehow it did. 'I'm fine,' she said putting her overnight bag on the floor and taking off her coat.

She'd wanted Steve to be with her but he'd gone to park the car. She felt flat and let down, desperately tired as she'd slept badly despite the clinic's routine sleeping pill.

It had been a largely silent journey home. She dozed in the back of the car either asleep or pretending to sleep. She didn't want to say anything, couldn't think of anything to say.

It had been a very strange experience and now here she was back home, not sure whether she was pregnant with Tina and Steve's embryo, or whether she would lose it.

Fearful of a multiple birth, they had all insisted on only one embryo being implanted, and the chances of this being successful were about twenty per cent even in someone young, fit and healthy like Louise.

If it failed would she try again?

Taking a glance at Tina's troubled face she thought that probably the answer would be 'no'.

'You know,' Tina carefully peeled off her gloves and threw them on the table, 'you're very welcome to come and live at the house if you'd like to. We're anxious to take care of you. I know people would talk, but so what? They'll find out sooner or later anyway.'

In fact, what the estate workers and villagers would think of this bizarre situation had not yet been addressed.

'No. No thank you,' Louise smiled. 'Not yet anyway. Maybe nearer the time?'

Tina plonked herself down in a chair looking so weary it was impossible not to feel sorry for her.

'Louise, I can't thank you enough for all you've done. I am, we both are, sincerely grateful. I know it was an ordeal. It was for us too, but worse for you. I don't think any of us realised how much was involved, all those beastly tests and examinations. Hopefully it will all be worth it.' She threw back her head and gave a brave smile. It was obvious that she had suffered. Oh, yes, she'd suffered.

'Well, we'll know in a couple of weeks.' Louise felt drained, overwhelmed with exhaustion. All she wanted to do was lie down and sleep.

'Louise,' Tina continued earnestly, 'I do want you to know how supportive we intend to be, Steve and I. Anything you need you have only to ask. Only work when you feel like it. I want you . . .' she stood up and attempted to put an arm round Louise's shoulder, 'I want you to try and think of me as a sister. Can you try and do that?'

'I'll try,' Louise said, but she did not sound convincing. 'Honestly, though, I don't want anything to change. I feel perfectly healthy and I want things to be just as they were before. Nothing *is* different you know.'

* * *

But everything was different. Steve felt different, very different. He knew Tina did too.

Back at the house Steve had helped himself to a whisky and looked anxiously at Tina as she came in.

'Is she OK? She was very silent in the car.'

'She's tired.' Tina took the drink he held out to her. 'Understandably.' She flopped into a chair and pushed back the lock of hair that had fallen over her forehead. 'But, oh dear, I sometimes wonder if we've done the right thing. If we should, perhaps, have gone to an agency, got someone we didn't know, who didn't live near us. Some stranger, you know . . . it might have been better.'

'But the whole point was that we *knew* Louise,' Steve said tetchily. 'Knew she was clean and wholesome, knew her mother, her background. I would never have consented to a stranger, certainly not someone from an agency, bearing our child.

The beauty of Louise is that we know so much about her. We can look after her, *and* our child.'

Tina appeared unconvinced.

'But, darling, Louise is such an *odd* girl. Sometimes I think I don't really know her myself and that somehow she resents me. I've tried my very best with her but she *is* difficult. Even over this she has been silent and mysterious. Not a bit forthcoming.'

Steve got up and helped himself to another drink. Then he went across to the window and spoke with his back to his wife.

'Darling, I think you're being *most* unreasonable. I don't think you've really tried to understand Louise. She is a very private person, restrained . . .'

'You mean I'm not?' Tina asked sharply.

'Not in the way that Louise is. Different, that's all.' He turned to face her. 'Louise has done a magnificent thing. An act of pure generosity. I don't think *I* could have contemplated it if I'd known what we were going to have to go through. All those tests! Personal examinations of the most intimate kind. Would you have done all that for someone else?'

'No,' Tina sat back, crossing her legs. 'Definitely not. I don't know *why* she's done it. I've said that before and I'll say it again. I only hope she won't make things difficult for us once the baby is born.'

'She can't. She's signed an agreement . . .'

'But people get out of these things. The baby will legally be hers until we adopt it.'

'Louise would never do a thing like that. I'm surprised you could even consider it. Besides, she knows she'd never win. No, it couldn't possibly come to that. I have every faith in Louise, even if you haven't. She's a friend, a brick, and we must give her all the support we can!' Steve perched on the arm of Tina's chair and planted a kiss on her forehead. 'This is something we must all share in together. Please Tina. Banish your doubts and fears. This must be a happy time, as having a baby should be . . . an occasion for joy. Trust Louise.'

*   *   *

Louise knew the implantation had taken even before the blood test two weeks later. One morning she woke up feeling queasy and the next day was the same. She supposed she had been hoping it wouldn't, but now, having gone so far . . . well it was something she wanted. Too late to back out.

But she wanted Steve to be the first to know. To share the moment of intimacy just with him, as if she could pretend to herself that it was their child, like any normal parents, and Tina could be excluded.

That day the architect came again to survey the site having already drawn up advance plans. Planning permission from the local authority was shortly expected. There was no sign of opposition. On the contrary the general view seemed to be that this would be a good thing for the area, attract more visitors, create more jobs.

Tina had gone to London to collect the children who now spent holidays with their father and term-time with their mother. Louise was a little late opening the shop because the nausea persisted, and she arrived feeling cold and washed out in keeping with the blustery March day.

Shortly afterwards Steve appeared with the

architect, both smiling.

'Planning permission should be through any time,' he said to Louise. 'Then full speed ahead. I'm taking Jeremy into the café to have a cup of coffee. Is anyone there yet?'

'Susan should be there.' Louise glanced through the door, looking for the catering manager, and shook her head. 'But she's not. Well, we don't really open until eleven. I can get you coffee if you want.'

Beckoning she preceded them through the door that led into the café.

'That's very kind of you, Louise.' Steve lightly put a hand on her shoulder. 'Everything OK? You look a little peaky.'

'It's a bit cold in here.' Louise rubbed her hands and went behind the counter. 'Take a seat. Coffee won't be long, but it will be instant I'm afraid.'

'Instant is fine,' Jeremy King said amiably, also rubbing his hands. 'Something wet and warm.'

'Come and join us, Louise,' Steve called out to her. 'The plans are looking really great.'

'I've a lot to do in the stock-room,' Louise shook her head. 'Maybe I'll see you later?'

The stock-room always provided such a good excuse. One could lose oneself, as she frequently did and knew that sometimes Tina did too. All those stacks and boxes and cupboards provided a bolt hole, a place of refuge.

'Sure,' Steve smiled at her as she placed two cups of coffee and a plate of biscuits in front of them. 'I'll show you the plans after Jeremy has gone.'

With Easter approaching there was a lot to do. Steve talked of getting more help, and Louise thought it would be needed. With the children now home for the holidays Tina had less time for the shop. The question was, who?

With the door of the stock-room slightly open Louise made herself comfortable on a chair and began a fresh inventory. She was absorbed in her work and the hand on her shoulder startled her.

'Are you OK?' Steve's voice was very close to her ear, his breath warm on her cheek. Startled she turned and his face was closer to her than it had ever been. She wanted to take it between her hands and kiss it. She wondered if the raw, naked emotion, the desire, showed in her eyes.

'Are you OK?' he said again. 'You look very pale.'

This was the moment of togetherness, the moment they should be sharing. For her to say 'our baby' and mean it was hers too.

'I think it's taken,' she said. 'I've been feeling sick all week.'

'Oh Louise, *darling* . . .' Steve pressed his cheek against hers, kissed her, held her there and then thrust her away and stared at her, his eyes gleaming. 'Tina will be so thrilled.'

'Are *you* thrilled?'

'Of course. But are you sure?'

'I have to have a blood test. But I'm pretty sure. I've never felt sick in the morning before, never the slightest bit queasy. Also, I feel terribly tired.'

'It's a miracle!' Steve exclaimed, almost to himself. 'They warned us it might not take. Said it was dodgy; they should have implanted several embryos. You're a miracle Louise!' He gazed at her admiringly. 'You're *the* miracle,' and then he bent to kiss her again.

83

As he did she turned her head abruptly so that their faces touched, their lips met. She wanted to cling to him, receive an answering embrace. She needed to tell him that she did love him and wanted his baby, that part of him was inside her, and she had done it so that she could be bonded with him. Wouldn't something of her be inside the child? Wouldn't she feed it with her placenta?

But Steve pulled violently away from her and looked at her strangely.

'Are you OK?'

'Sorry,' she gulped. 'Not feeling terribly good today. I think I'll go home.'

'I'll take you and make sure you're alright. Shall I call the doctor?'

'Oh, no. No need for that. But what about the shop?'

'We'll close the shop until you feel better. Your health is what matters. We really do need to get someone else. Tina will be too busy with the children.'

Then tenderly he led her into the shop and sat her down on a chair.

'Now, you wait here while I get the car. We have to take care of you. You're very precious, you know.'

*　　　*　　　*

She *was* very precious and he'd called her 'darling'. It had been spontaneous and he may not have intended to say it, just yet. Nevertheless he had. She had touched his lips, felt their firm pressure. The baby inside her was working its miracle, as somehow she thought it would.

Things never could, never should be the same again.

Louise sat for a long time after Steve had gone thinking about him, sorry no longer about what had happened. All the long process, the tests, the examinations, the fears and uncertainty were in the past, vindicated now by the revelation of Steve's feelings for her.

It was no longer a matter of self-deception. It was real. How much better it would have been if Steve had told Tina how he felt about her, and he and Louise could have had their own child in the normal way.

Tina might not have understood, might have been hurt, even deeply wounded but she was a beautiful woman and would easily attract another partner. She was really quite superficial, without any depth and would soon get over losing Steve. The extent of her shallowness was shown by the fact that she would allow another woman to bear her child! How desperate she must have been to want to keep her man.

It was not as though Steve would be discarding the old and unwanted wife. It was not cruel to Tina. It was much more cruel to continue with this pretence. But then Steve might never have faced up to his true feelings if this hadn't happened. Louise knew now for certain that he felt very close to her, had wanted her to bear his child.

As for her and Tina thinking of themselves as sisters . . . The notion was farcical.

Louise roused herself from her reverie and went into the kitchen to make a cup of tea. As she did there was a knock on the front door and Buddy put his head round.

'Hi!' he said.

'Hi. Come in. I'm just making a cup of tea.'

Buddy carefully closed the door behind him. He followed her into the kitchen and watched her making the tea. Glancing up at him she thought his face looked strained.

She made two mugs of tea, added milk and sugar and put them with a plate of biscuits on a tray which Buddy carried into the sitting room.

'You look very solemn,' Louise said, sitting down on the couch and carefully putting her feet up. 'Anything wrong?'

Buddy took his mug and a biscuit from the plate and sat down opposite Louise.

'I know you'll say it's none of my business,' he said, in a strained voice. 'But I happened to see Steve coming out of here a few minutes ago.'

'So?' Louise, her expression hardening, looked across at him.

'Are you having an affair?'

'You're right, it is none of your business.'

'But I want to know . . .' Buddy put his mug firmly on the table and got up.

'But you said it was none of your business.'

'Nevertheless it is. I am very fond of you, and I think if you are carrying on with Steve, as I've told you before, you're making a terrible mistake. This could lead to all sorts of trouble . . .'

Louise carefully put her mug down and wiped her biscuity fingers on a hanky.

'It already has. I'm pregnant.'

'Oh my God!' Buddy flopped back in his chair and buried his face in his hands.

'That's why I've been away so often.'

'It's Steve's baby?'

86

'Of course.' Louise looked at him smugly. 'I told you he cared about me.'

'It doesn't mean he cares about you, you silly woman,' Buddy said savagely. 'He just wanted to screw you.'

'That's a horrible thing to say,' Louise's tone was icy.

'I'm sorry,' Buddy said, suddenly contrite. 'I didn't mean it that way. It's only that I'm very upset. You know how I feel about you. It seems now that there is no hope . . . never was, I suppose?' He looked at her wanly and she shook her head.

'I'm *so* sorry Buddy. I really am. I like you so much, as a friend, but it was always Steve. You knew that.'

'I didn't think he really cared for you and you were deluding yourself.' Buddy paused. 'Does Tina know?'

'What do you think?'

'I suppose not. But what are you going to do when she finds out?'

'I think I'll tell her it's yours,' Louise said with a sudden mischievous smile. 'What do you think about that? She thinks we have a relationship anyway. This will prove it. That way everyone will be happy.'

CHAPTER SIX

Tina watched the children holding tightly onto the roundabout in the playground near Poynton village school. They were the only children on it as it was still term time for the local schoolchildren, whereas those such as Bethany and William, who went to private schools, had much longer holidays.

Tina would be very glad when the holidays were over, although they had only just begun and it seemed like a lifetime stretching ahead of her. She supposed that they were no more difficult than most children of their age, and yet they seemed to give her an especially hard time. They always had, as if they resented the fact that their father had married her.

It was very difficult to love them, to feel, indeed, any affection for them because of this barrier of hostility that they had created from the start.

Frances was dark and William took after her: jet black hair, deep blue eyes, a very handsome, even beautiful boy, very tall for his age. Bethany, two years older, had Steve's corn-coloured hair, clear complexion, keen, disconcertingly direct blue eyes. She too was unusually tall, and even at twelve she was stunning looking, with the composure of a much older girl. She could pass for fifteen or so.

It always seemed to Tina that William would have been more inclined to be friendly were it not for Bethany who disliked the very idea of her stepmother. But William was easily led. He was softer, gentler than his sister, but always fell in with her wishes.

Tina thought it would be a good thing when they both went to boarding school which was the idea for the autumn as even their natural mother found them a handful too.

They were so easily bored and there was nothing more boring on a mild summer's afternoon than to go round and round on a roundabout, a plaything for babies.

Tina looked at her watch and hailed them for about the third or fourth time, but they took no notice. Tina even fancied that Bethany stuck her tongue out at her, but it might have been the whizzing of the merry-go-round that deceived her.

She rubbed her eyes hard. She was tired. She was also nervous and ill at ease. The holidays were a testing time, and with the sort of year she'd had it made the situation all the more difficult.

This time next year she'd have her own child and, hopefully, after a year at boarding school Bethany might have grown up a little, though she considered herself very grown-up now.

Was this why she had so much wanted a child of her own? It was a chilly day and Tina wandered back to the car to wait for the children who, after protesting at the very idea of going to the playground, now didn't want to leave it and ignored her summonses to come to the car.

At one time to have a child of her own had seemed the be all and end all of life. It might help her to see her stepchildren in a different light and cement her bond with Steve. So, with a desperation born of failure, she'd accepted Louise's offer.

But now that Louise was actually carrying the child, she wished that somehow she had resisted because it didn't seem like her child at all. It seemed like Louise's, and Louise made her feel that way.

Louise had said she didn't want anything to change, but everything had changed. Steve had changed. He paid an awful lot of attention to Louise which was really quite unnatural, as well as unnecessary, because after all pregnancy wasn't a disease.

The more attention Steve paid to Louise the more Tina drew away from her and the more isolated she felt. That dreaded sense of insecurity, of things slipping away began to haunt her again.

Yet Louise was only three months' pregnant. Another six months seemed an awful long time to wait.

Bethany and William finally came, with obvious reluctance, to the car and got into the back. Without saying a word Tina drew away from the playground and headed towards home.

'Are you cross?' Bethany asked when they were halfway there.

'No. Why should I be?'

'You seem cross.'

'I just don't like children being disobedient. I must have asked you six times if you would get ready to come home and you ignored me.' She half turned her head towards Bethany. 'Besides it sets a very bad example to William, who always imitates you.'

'I don't,' William retorted.

'Well, I think you do.'

'It's just because you don't like us,' Bethany said to Tina's back. 'You hate us.'

Tina abruptly stopped the car just inside the gates, within sight of the house, and turned to face them.

'I don't dislike you. I certainly don't *hate* you. I simply don't understand you. Why, when you have the best of all worlds do you want to be unpleasant? I do my utmost to make you happy while you're here and I fail every time. What more can I do?'

90

'We were only sent to Mummy because you couldn't cope with us.'

'That is not true,' Tina said angrily. 'I wasn't in very good health. I had awful migraines. Luckily, with new medication I'm better. It's more under control.'

'Then why can't we come back and be with you and Daddy?' Bethany wailed.

'Would you want to?'

Bethany lowered her eyes beneath Tina's fierce gaze.

'I understood you wanted to go to boarding school and that's what's going to happen. I understood it was put to you and you agreed. No one is trying to get rid of you, neither your mother and father nor I. Personally I think boarding school is an excellent idea. You make lots of friends, and holidays seem so exciting.'

'Were you at boarding school?'

'No.'

'How do you know then?'

'Because I heard. I would have liked to have gone to boarding school as a matter of fact but my parents couldn't afford it. You're very privileged and you don't seem to realise it.'

Bethany leaned her arms over the seat in front of her with a malicious look in her eyes, and as Tina turned to restart the car she stuck her tongue out at her behind her back.

When they got back to the house the children scrambled out of the car without so much as a 'thank you' or a backward glance. Angrily Tina drove round to garage the car noting that Steve was also home.

Reluctant to face the children again she walked

down the drive to the garden centre and was surprised to find that, despite the crowd of people milling around, the door to the shop was shut and locked.

She went through the side gate into the garden and saw a rather harassed Duncan taking money for plants on an improvised table.

'Where's Louise?' Tina asked during a lull. 'Why is the place shut up?'

'Louise is not well,' Duncan grunted wiping his perspiring brow with the back of his hand. 'Your husband took her back to the cottage.'

He gave Tina a canny look which plunged her immediately into a state of indecision, not knowing whether to open the shop or appear too anxious to go and see what was wrong with Louise. She had her mind made up for her when Duncan said he hadn't the key, Louise must have taken it with her. A spare one was up at the house.

Tina set off for Louise's cottage in the village, her emotions a jumble of foreboding mixed with hope.

After all, if Louise were to have a miscarriage wouldn't it be the best solution? She quickened her steps and as she came in sight of the cottage saw another car parked outside the gate. As she approached the door it opened and Steve appeared talking earnestly to Dr Martin.

'I just heard,' Tina said nervously brushing back her hair. 'How is she?'

'Touch and go,' the doctor grimaced. 'We will know in the next day or two if she's going to lose the baby. All she can do now is rest, and then we'll do an ultrasound and check her hormone levels. Maybe you'd like to go back to the clinic to be sure?'

'We'll ask Louise.' Steve sounded worried and, after shaking the doctor's hand, hurried back inside the cottage without waiting for Tina.

'You're not very happy about this are you, Tina?' Dr Martin said in a low voice.

'About what?' She followed him as he walked slowly back to the car.

'The whole thing. If you'd asked me I would have advised against it.'

'Too late now,' Tina said glancing back at the cottage as if she was afraid they were being observed.

'Maybe not. If she miscarries . . . and I do think it looks likely. Tell me, does Steve want this baby so much?'

'It seems like it,' Tina murmured. 'It was done for *my* sake but . . . Oh,' as if afraid of saying too much she smiled bleakly at the doctor. 'I'd better go inside and see what's happening there.'

'Anyway, the headaches are better?'

'Oh, much better.'

'Maybe there was a connection?'

'I don't know what you mean?' Tina frowned.

'Wanting the baby . . .'

'Oh, I see. I thought it was the medicine you gave me.'

She saw the doctor into his car, waved him off and then walked back to the cottage. He had been trying to insinuate that he thought her migraine had been psychological. What wasn't these days?

She could hear voices from upstairs and was tempted for a moment to stay where she was. However, eventually she climbed the stairs from where, when she got to the top, she could see Steve

93

sitting on the side of Louise's bed holding her hand.

'I tell you, you mustn't worry,' he was saying as Tina entered the room.

'I don't want to disappoint you,' Louise whispered and Tina noticed how tightly she was clasping Steve's hand.

As Tina gritted her teeth Steve looked up and saw her.

She went over to the bed and looked at the recumbent woman. She was, indeed, very pale.

'How do you feel?' she asked.

'I feel alright now. I just noticed some blood when I went to the loo. I was in the shop. Steve was with Duncan. He said I should go home and called the doctor on his mobile.'

'She has to rest. He said it's not all that unusual at three months, but she should have a scan and some tests.'

'He told me,' Tina nodded. 'Is there anything I can do? Would you like a cup of tea?'

'Tea would be lovely.' Louise nodded, still hanging onto Steve's hand.

Feeling inadequate, glad to escape the cloying scene, Tina went downstairs and made three mugs of tea, found an open packet of biscuits and put the lot on the tray, carefully taking them upstairs.

Louise's eyes were now closed. 'I think she's asleep,' Steve whispered. He got up and took his mug over to the window, Tina following him. 'It's an awful trauma for her. We can't leave her. I think one of us should stay the night.'

'You think that's really necessary?'

'Of course it's necessary.' He looked at her with surprise. 'She might be miscarrying your baby . . .'

94

Tina said nothing but stood sipping her tea gazing out of the window. She was aware that Steve's expression was critical.

'Don't you care?' he asked.

'Of course I care.' Tina glanced at the sleeping woman wondering if she really was asleep or just pretending. 'I . . .' she stopped as she heard the sound of footsteps hurrying up the stairs and a second later Buddy appeared at the door. He immediately crossed over to Louise and bent and looked at her. Steve put a finger to his lips.

'She's asleep.'

'Is she alright?'

Steve pointed to the door, took up the tray and the three of them crept silently out of the room.

'Would you like a cup of tea?' Tina asked as they stood in an awkward huddle downstairs rather as if they didn't know what to say.

'No thank you.' Buddy stared belligerently at Steve, clearly very angry.

'What is wrong with Louise? I heard she had to go home.'

Steve looked across at Tina whose eyes fastened on Buddy.

'She had a threatened miscarriage. I suppose she told you she's pregnant?'

'Yes, she told me.' Buddy's face was pale with anger. 'I think it's absolutely outrageous.' He stared accusingly at Tina. 'I wonder *you're* not angry too.'

'Angry?' Tina looked puzzled. 'Why should I be angry? Concerned but not angry.'

'Then you obviously condone the whole thing?'

'How do you mean "condone"?' Now it was Tina's turn to boil over. 'It was something Louise agreed to, offered to do. There was no compulsion on our part, though I must say at times I am sorry we ever went in for it.'

Buddy scratched his head, anger suddenly replaced by bewilderment and sat down next to Tina.

'I don't know what's going on. Please explain. Louise offered to do *what*?'

'Oh, then she hasn't told you . . .' Tina's voice faltered.

'She told me she was pregnant and Steve was the father.'

'Ah,' Tina glanced triumphantly across at Steve, 'you thought she was pregnant by my husband and I knew nothing about it?'

'I assumed they were having an affair. That's what she led me to believe.'

'Which we certainly were not.' Steve looked indignantly at Buddy. 'Louise *agreed* to be a surrogate mother as Tina was unable to carry a child. The baby she is expecting is ours. We never asked her. It was her idea. She offered voluntarily and at the time it seemed a good idea.'

'You don't think it's a good idea now?' Buddy looked from one to the other.

'As I said sometimes I have my doubts,' Tina said. 'I'm not sure about Steve.'

'We wanted someone we knew and liked. We considered Louise like a member of the family. She saw a programme on surrogacy on the TV and she offered. We thought a lot about it. We had tests. We all had psychiatric counselling. Finally we went along with the whole thing.'

'I find this quite unbelievable,' Buddy rubbed his face wearily.

'Sometimes I do too,' Steve said. 'It has had drawbacks but, as I said, it seemed a good idea at the time.'

'How did you feel when she told you she was pregnant?' Tina asked curiously.

'Angry. I am very fond of her. I wished the child had been mine. Frankly I thought Steve was a bastard. I'm sorry. I didn't know.'

*   *   *

For a long time they sat silently in the car without speaking. Buddy gripped the wheel, his eyes concentrating on the road. Louise sat hunched up, thoughtful. She'd wanted Steve to bring her, but Buddy offered and it was difficult to turn him down.

'Do you feel very cross with me?' she asked at last.

'I feel sorry for you.' Buddy spoke without looking at her. 'To do such a *stupid* thing. What could you possibly gain from it?'

'I wanted to help them.'

'*Them*? You wanted to help Tina too?'

'Of course.' Louise glanced at him. 'Why not?'

'I thought you didn't like her.'

'I don't dislike her.'

'Isn't she your rival for Steve's affections?'

'She's his wife, not my rival. You're talking a lot of drivel Buddy. I wish I hadn't let you drive me.'

'I want to try and talk some sense into you. Look,' they were in a country lane on their way to the clinic and Buddy slowed down, 'you have a threatened miscarriage. Why not let nature take its course?'

97

'You mean *lose* the baby?'

'Yes. Why not?'

'Because I promised Steve and Tina.'

'If you ask me they're having second thoughts. Tina especially seems not so keen on the idea.'

'Steve wants the baby,' Louise said stubbornly.

'I think you're sick,' Buddy speeded up. 'I really think you should see a psychiatrist.'

'I have,' Louise said smugly. 'We all saw psychiatrists, doctors, psychologists, counsellors, you name it. We saw the lot. They think I'm perfectly sane. A lot of women become surrogates and for different reasons. Some are strangers and both parties prefer it that way. Some are friends or relations. It's much more common than you think.'

'But did *you* want a baby?'

'Not particularly. I wanted to help Steve and Tina.'

'You wanted to help *Steve*. You wanted to be impregnated with his child so that you could get at him.'

'I think *you're* the one who's sick,' Louise retorted. 'I don't want to discuss it any more,' and she tried to curl herself up into a ball in the seat and pretended to go to sleep.

*   *   *

Janice sat by the side of the sleeping woman, her face thoughtful. Sensing her presence Louise's eyelids fluttered and she opened them.

'Goodness, what time is it?'

'It's alright. It's only seven.'

'I was tired.' Louise stretched in the bed. 'It's been such a harrowing time.'

98

'Still, you're perfectly OK. The ultrasound showed just a bit of bleeding behind the placenta which it has nearly absorbed.'

'Why does this happen?'

'Sometimes it does.' Janice shrugged. 'But if you want to go ahead with the baby you should rest for a few days. Take it easy. I mean not here, but at home. Oh, Steve rang. I told him that everything was perfectly alright.'

Louise gazed at the ceiling. She'd wished so much Steve had come. She was sure Tina had stopped him.

'Steve and Tina didn't come with you?' Janice asked as if reading her mind.

'It's complicated.'

'I expect it is . . . and the man you brought with you?'

'A kind of friend.'

'A "kind of friend"?' Janice's tone was sarcastic.

'I don't see what business it is of yours.'

'It is not my business.' Janice pulled up a chair and sat down beside her. 'But he seems very fond of you. Concerned. What does worry me, and in a way concerns me too as the doctor in charge of your case, is that this appears to be a very complex situation and I fear someone is going to get hurt. That means the child that you're carrying as well as everyone else.'

'But don't you think about this aspect before you carry out these procedures? It strikes me it must always be a complex situation.'

'Yes it is and that's why we counsel people and try and examine their motives. I was always a bit unhappy about you, but Dr Marsden overruled me. He felt it was a healthy relationship between you,

Tina and Steve. I wasn't so sure. I thought Tina and Steve might bring you here today. Natural parents usually do. Are things not so good between you and them?'

'Tina's not terribly happy. Steve is so concerned about me. I think she's jealous.'

'This often is the case. But more often when the surrogate mother is also the egg donor. That can lead to real complications.'

'But in this case it's her baby too . . .'

'Maybe she doesn't see it that way.'

'I'll be glad when it's all over,' Louise said and then suddenly, unexpectedly, she burst into tears.

*   *   *

Buddy wondered that people should make life so complicated when really it was so simple. He was a simple man with simple tastes, not in the sense that he was stupid. He was very far from that.

His parents had both died when he was young and he had been raised by his grandparents who had taught him independence and self-sufficiency. His grandfather had been a farmer and when he died he left the farm to Buddy who sold most of the stock, except the hens, and started to grow vegetables for sale to local markets based entirely on the principles of organic cultivation, without the use of artificial fertilisers or pesticides.

It was hard work making this viable until gradually organic produce began to be popular and people were seen to be prepared to pay extra for it.

He still wasn't a wealthy man but he owned the farm and a hundred acres of land, all under cultivation. He had begun to establish outlets in

London and some of his produce was now ferried there weekly by lorry.

Buddy had not been immediately attracted to Louise when she came to live permanently with her mother. He found her rather withdrawn, almost unfriendly and, at first, was inclined to put her down as a woman who did not like men. But when her mother died her attitude towards him changed. He helped with the funeral preparations, the winding up of the estate. She came to depend on him and he felt her confidence in him increasing. As she grew more relaxed with him he began to realise how attractive she was, not conventionally pretty but handsome. She was also very capable and there dawned on him the possibility of a life together and with it the hope that in time this would come about.

This hope had been doomed to disappointment once he found out about Steve.

However, rather as Louise held onto the conviction that one day Steve would leave Tina and turn to her, Buddy continued to hope that a similar dramatic change of circumstances would deliver Louise up to him.

Louise had spent the night in the clinic just for a rest and more tests following the ultrasound scan. Buddy stayed at a hotel where he found himself with plenty of time to consider not only the present, but the future. Now he sat in the vestibule of the clinic looking at the daily paper, rather than reading it, glancing up every few seconds to see if there was any sign of Louise.

Finally she appeared through the door with the dark haired woman doctor he had met the day before by her side carrying her overnight bag. She smiled at Buddy who stood up, his gaze resting anxiously upon Louise.

'Everything's fine,' she said. 'No complications.'

'Good,' Buddy studied Louise's tense face. 'Shall we go then?'

'You're to telephone me or come back if you have any worries.' Janice looked earnestly at Louise. 'Promise?'

'I promise,' Louise said as Buddy took her bag then, impulsively, she leaned forward and kissed Janice on the cheek. 'And thanks.'

'Seems like a nice lady,' Buddy said as they walked to the car.

'She is. They're all very nice. She said most people have problems with surrogacy.'

'So, you still feel you've got problems?' Buddy opened the car door for Louise, who tucked herself inside. Then he went round to the driver's seat and started the engine.

'Of course,' Louise said looking steadily ahead, 'it's one hell of a big problem.'

Buddy switched off the engine. 'Didn't you think it might be at the beginning?'

'Well . . . I knew it wouldn't be *easy*. I wanted to do it for Steve, and Tina of course. But I forgot about the morning sickness, the exhaustion, the complications. I mean, I might die.'

'Seems unlikely,' Buddy said with a nervous laugh.

'No, seriously. I mean it is not likely but it could happen.'

Buddy's expression turned to one of anxiety. 'But Janice doesn't think it's likely, does she?'

'Oh no. No one does. This bleeding is quite common and in all respects I am very healthy. But I don't think I thought about carrying somebody else's baby *inside* me. I mean it's *part* of me. If it was just Steve . . . it would be alright.'

'You mean if it was your baby and Steve's?'

'Yes.' Louise joined her hands and gazed down at her lap. 'I suppose that is what I do feel. It has been so awkward with Tina. She isn't natural with me. It's affecting Steve.'

'Do you think it might be better if you went away?' Buddy said gently.

Immediately Louise looked terrified.

'Went *away*? Are you *serious*? Where on earth could I go? What would I do? And when the baby is born what do I do then? Stay away? Why should I leave my home just for them?' She paused and then said gravely, 'If anyone should go it's Tina. Not me. Without Tina everything in the garden would be lovely.'

CHAPTER SEVEN

Bethany pressed her nose to the window gazing disconsolately out at the pouring rain.

'I wish it wouldn't *rain* so much,' she moaned. 'I wish we were abroad with Mummy and George.'

'It strikes me you always want something you haven't got,' Steve ruffled her hair fondly. 'Would you like to go to the cinema?'

Bethany shrugged. 'Not much.'

'Well, what would you like to do? I'm afraid you can't go to Algiers. It's too far.'

He attempted to smile but he wasn't feeling happy. The children were a problem. He felt he was too busy and Tina found them a handful. You couldn't blame her because they were either rude to her or pretended she didn't exist.

It had been a fraught summer with many problems, not least of them the children. He would be glad when the time came to start school even though they were now protesting at the thought of boarding school.

The only person they really seemed happy with was Louise. They spent a lot of time with her, had days out with her while Tina looked after the shop, assisted now by a young recruit from the village called Ruth who was waiting to go to university.

The summer had been a busy one for Steve. As soon as planning permission came through, Duncan's cottage had been razed to the ground and the foundations were now being laid for the new hotel.

A trip to Bermuda *en famille* had been on the cards, but was cancelled due to some last-minute hitches to the hotel plans, so that the children had much time on their hands. William was quite happy playing games on the computer, but Bethany hung around sulking about not going to Bermuda, finding one source of dissatisfaction after another.

She was difficult to entertain, and even trying to make her useful doing things in the shop proved a disaster. She, ostensibly accidentally, knocked over a carefully arranged table full of porcelain plates, cups and saucers and did two and a half thousand pounds' worth of damage. After that she was kept well away which was probably what she wanted.

She enjoyed riding, and Steve would go riding with her, usually in the morning, but neither Tina nor Louise rode, so this form of entertainment was limited.

After the scare of Louise's miscarriage there were no more alarms and the tenor of life at Poynton had settled down, Louise keeping to her promise that she wanted things to be 'normal'. Indeed it was almost possible to believe that nothing had changed. As long as Louise remained well, and she did, the baby was scarcely discussed. It was as though the three of them had settled into their roles of prospective parents, rather, Steve felt, as when Bethany and William were on the way, like a normal fact of life.

But now, at five months, Louise's pregnancy was becoming obvious. There were people making remarks about her increase in weight. There was, above all, the problem of what to tell the children, an issue they all appeared to have shelved.

'Shall I call Louise up from the shop?' Steve asked. 'You'd like that wouldn't you?'

'Oh yes,' Bethany brightened at once. 'Louise always thinks of something to do.'

'Even on a rainy day?' Steve smiled.

'Louise *always* thinks of something to do,' Bethany repeated then looked gravely at her father. 'I wish you'd married *Louise* instead of Tina. Why didn't you when you had the chance?'

'Because I didn't love Louise,' Steve replied. 'I loved Tina and still do, very much.'

'But Louise is much nicer.'

'That's not true, darling.' Steve drew her gently to him. 'I mean Louise is nice, and we all like her, but liking someone and being in love is different as you'll find out when you grow up. Do you really think if I'd married Louise you'd have liked her as much as you do? Isn't it, perhaps, that you're trying

105

to get your own back on Tina for marrying me?'

'How do you mean?' Bethany asked sulkily.

'By making life difficult for her. You'd rather I hadn't married anyone. You wanted Mummy and me to stay together. Well, so did I. Mummy left me, not the other way round. I was very lonely after she'd gone and then Tina and I got together. Tina has done her very best to be a good second mother to you and all the reward she gets is rudeness. If you want to make me happy will you try and be as nice to Tina as you are to Louise?'

Bethany continued to gaze at him mulishly and, knowing that he would get nowhere, Steve went to the phone and pressed the button that connected the house with the shop. It was answered by Tina.

'Is Louise there, darling?'

'Yes, do you want to talk to her?'

'I wondered if she could come and entertain the children. They're bored, at least Bethany is. Can you spare her?'

'Well,' Tina paused, 'we're not very busy. It's so wet. I'll have a word with her. I think she's in the stock-room.'

*   *   *

Tina put down the phone and looked round for Louise. There was hardly anyone in the shop but there were a few people in the café. Louise appeared at the door of the stock-room her arms full of cards.

'We shall soon have to start thinking of Christmas,' she said putting them down on the counter.

'Oh surely not?' Tina looked at her in alarm. 'It's

106

not yet autumn.'

'Nevertheless people begin preparing for Christmas early.' Louise bent to pick up a box from the floor and Tina hurried round to help her.

'Here, let me do that,' she said looking obliquely at Louise. 'You know, we shall have to decide what to tell people soon. The baby is beginning to show.'

'I know.' Louise straightened up, her hand on her back. 'I think most people must guess.' For a moment or two she studied Tina's face. 'I think tell them the truth, don't you? It's nothing to be ashamed of.'

Tina busied herself stacking the cards on the table, artistic impressions of the manor and the gardens.

'Steve phoned. He asked if you'd like to do something with the children.' Tina gazed out of the window at the pouring rain. 'I don't quite know what he has in mind. A drive maybe?' She frowned. 'I wish I got on with them as well as you do. I try but it's hard. Frankly I shall be glad when it's time for them to go to school. We can then prepare ourselves . . .' Her gaze seemed to linger on Louise's stomach and she gave a wan smile. 'After all, as you say, Christmas is not so far away.'

Louise went back to the stock-room and emerged pulling on her coat. 'I'm glad I brought the car,' she said matter of factly. 'I'll drive up. Look . . . would you like me to say something to the children? You know . . .' she put a hand lightly against her stomach rather as though it was a word neither of them liked to utter.

'Oh no,' Tina shook her head. 'You'd better leave that to me and Steve. We've got to decide on the right moment, the right thing to say. Maybe it

107

might be better left until the baby is born. After all you're going away and they needn't see you again. It might not even be necessary for them to know that you're pregnant. I mean . . . might it?' She looked rather lamely at Louise.

'But a baby can't just "appear",' Louise retorted. 'It's quite obvious that *you're* not pregnant, so where will they think it came from? Under the cabbage bush?'

She turned on her heels and Tina, conscious of her gaffe, stood watching her as she crossed the courtyard to the car park and climbed into her car.

She had offended Louise and once again she hadn't meant to. The tension between them was always there beneath the surface however hard they tried to paper over it. Days, even weeks went by without incident and then some little thing blew up and Louise went into a huff. It was quite natural Tina supposed. She had always found her volatile and unpredictable even when she wasn't pregnant, quick to take offence, see slurs, slights on her character where none were intended. Louise was really a complex character. Her apparant common sense contrasted so oddly with her swift changes of mood. She was perceived as sensible, down-to-earth. In reality she was anything but.

Tina now thought she was rather dangerous and hoped nothing of her personality transferred itself to the baby. One thing was very clear: she doted on Steve, maybe thought he should have married Louise instead of her.

The question was what would happen after the baby was born? Would Louise relinquish control easily or would she regard herself as a second mother? Would she ingratiate herself with the growing child as she did with Bethany and William? None of them had faced up to that even though the counsellors at the clinic had tried to make them.

'It will be alright,' they had said, Louise being such a close friend of the family, a person everyone liked and trusted.

*   *   *

Louise drove furiously up to the house, splashing through the puddles on the drive in a terrible rage against Tina. Most of the time she managed to suppress her true feelings behind a veneer but it was becoming increasingly difficult.

The more conscious she had become of the baby; the first movements, the awareness of its presence made her feel that the child was really hers, not Tina's at all. It seemed so unfair to think of giving it up, of watching it grow, being on the sidelines as—what? Some sort of aunt or glorified nanny in a patronising way, as the family regarded her now. She was like a milch cow without a will, a mind or a body of her own. When all else fails send for Louise, she won't mind.

She parked her car behind the house and ran to the shelter of the porch, pausing outside long enough to catch her breath. Through the window she could see Steve talking to Bethany with such a sweet, patient smile on his face that her anger evaporated and heart went out to him.

Steve, after all, the gentlest, kindest of men, was really like a single parent for all the support he got from his wife. Here he was on a rainy afternoon with a thousand important things to do and at his wit's end not knowing how to entertain the children, poor darling. And he had sent for her not Tina, knowing how useless Tina would be.

She stood for a moment gazing at him, seeing but not being seen, such was his concentration on his daughter. Really, he was caught in a trap, always having to think of other people: Tina who so wanted a baby, Bethany who was discontented with her life, too old for her age. Yet how much did Steve think about her? As merely an old pal, or something closer?

Louise took off her coat in the hall and quietly opened the door. Steve looked up, a smile of welcome on his face when he saw her. He jumped up to greet her and came over to her, arms extended.

'Ah, there you are, Louise. You see how indispensable you are? Everyone needs you. You're a darling. I knew I could depend on you.' The relief in his voice palpable, he took her arm, kissed her lightly on the cheek and looked at her almost tenderly. 'I promise I'll make it up to you. How are things at the shop?'

'Quiet,' Louise said as Bethany also ran over to her and seized her hand. 'What would you like to do?' she asked looking down at her. 'Play something? Go for a drive? Where's William?'

'Playing with his computer!' Bethany spluttered contemptuously. 'Games of course.'

'I think the rain's clearing,' Steve said, looking out of the window. 'I'd better go and see how that waterlogged building site is getting on. Now, while you decide what to do . . . Oh, Louise can I have a word?' Steve looked at her mysteriously and as he drew her to one side turned to his daughter. 'Bethany darling you go and get William.

Sometimes I'm sorry I ever bought him that computer.'

'And get your raincoat,' Louise called after Bethany as she sped to the door. 'Just in case.' She turned eagerly to Steve as he drew her down onto the sofa. Once again she was conscious of that sense of excitement, that quickening of the heartbeat, rare these days as she so seldom had him to herself.

'I want to ask you something,' he said lowering his voice though there was no one within earshot. 'It's about Tina. Well, she's had a very hard time of it recently. The children, especially Beth, are difficult, and I have been too busy with the complex and its attendant problems to help her out. We were going away but it wasn't possible. It just happens now that I've discovered a lull in the programme and on the spur of the moment I thought, as a surprise, I'd like to take Tina for a holiday somewhere. She deserves a break. I thought maybe Florida or the Bahamas. Do you think you could hold the fort? It won't be for long and we do so rely on you. The children are always so happy with you. I can fill you in with what the builders should be doing . . .' He stopped, aware that Louise was staring at him in a peculiar and unfamiliar way, her chin set stubbornly. 'You don't *mind* do you? You know what a brick you are.'

'Mind?' Louise muttered. 'No, of course not. Only *I* haven't had a holiday either and I've had a difficult year too. I don't expect you thought of that, did you Steve? Now I'm landed with the children, which of course I don't mind, and the building problems while you go off and enjoy yourselves. I am also nearly six months' pregnant and I do get very tired.'

Steve gave an embarrassed cough. 'Well, I can hardly ask you to come with us even if it was possible . . . who would look after the children?'

'I wouldn't *dream* of coming with you,' Louise said huffily. 'Such a notion never crossed my mind. It's simply that you seem to think Tina deserves a holiday rather more than me.'

'I think you do deserve a holiday, of course I do, especially, as you say . . .' Again with the apparent shyness that overcame them when it came to saying 'that word' he gazed at her stomach. 'And when it is all over you and Buddy shall go wherever you like at my expense. How about South Africa or the West Indies?'

'You mean I'm being exiled?'

'Of course I don't mean that. Louise don't be so sensitive.' Steve was alarmed by the change in Louise's tone and manner. 'Not at all. It will be just a way of saying "thank you" while Tina and I get to know our baby.'

'And why include Buddy?' Louise wanted to know.

'Well . . .' Steve seemed lost for words. 'I thought you'd like a companion.'

'Steve, sometimes I do think you really are crass,' Louise said completely losing her cool. 'Will you tell Bethany and William I'll be waiting for them in the car?'

*   *   *

Once again there was that feeling of rage, of being possessed by a seemingly uncontrollable force of indignation and resentment. Was there ever anyone

112

so ungrateful, so insensitive as those two? Waltzing off on holiday when she was entering the final period of a laborious process which, after all, she was doing for them.

The rage made her keep her foot down hard on the accelerator until Bethany, rather white-faced, said, 'Aren't you going a *bit* too quickly, Louise? Is anything wrong?'

Louise's hands were tightly gripping the wheel of the car as she slowed down.

'Sorry,' she said with a forced smile. 'Where do you want to go?'

'Nowhere in particular.' Bethany touched her arm in a gesture of affection. 'It's just nice being alone with you. It's nice with Daddy too, of course. Daddy and you, but not Tina . . .' She looked mischievously at Louise who failed to rise to the bait as she always did. She didn't think she'd ever uttered a word of criticism about Tina to the children, though perhaps something of her feelings inevitably showed in her manner.

'Look, if you like we can go to Montacute.' Louise referred to the stately home now in the care of the National Trust on the outskirts of Yeovil. 'We always like to have a look at the competition and we can have a cup of tea there.' 'The competition' meant keeping track of what was on offer at the shop, and what was being served in the restaurant.

Bethany pulled a face. She *was* difficult, Louise said to herself; rather an unhappy, spoilt little girl who it was, indeed, very hard to please. Moreover, she always liked to have her own way and managed to bend her brother to her will.

'I'd like to go to . . .' Bethany paused and

113

intently studied the roof of the car. 'Montacute!' she announced as if producing a rabbit from a hat.

'Glad you agree,' Louise gave a sigh of relief. 'Now that the rain appears to have stopped you can have a run round. Is Montacute alright for you, William?'

William who had been engrossed in his computer game and hadn't wanted to come out at all nodded glumly.

Her heart lifting slightly, Louise reversed the car and drove in the direction of the pretty village which gave its name to the large and very beautiful Elizabethan house, formerly the home of the Philips' family, who built and lived in it until they fell on hard times. It was also once the home of Lord Curzon, Viceroy of India.

It had many fine examples of seventeenth- and eighteenth- century English furniture and a long gallery containing Elizabethan and Jacobean portraits from the National Portrait Gallery in London. But these, of course, or the house itself, were of little interest to the children. Nevertheless as the rain cleared and the sun came out, the formal grounds of Montacute provided ample scope for them to run about after tea, while Louise, having inspected the shop and seen how many lines rivalled, if at all, those at Poynton, sat on a bench making notes. She kept her eye on Bethany and William playing hide and seek among the enchanting small open rotundas in the forecourt.

Finally, tiring, Bethany flopped down beside her.

'Why don't you come and play?'

'I'm a bit tired,' Louise said smiling at her. 'I also wanted to make some notes about the shop. Not as good as ours,' she said with an air of quiet

114

satisfaction, closing her book.

Bethany glanced at her slyly.

'Why are you tired?'

'Just am.' Louise put a hand to support her aching back. 'Sometimes my back hurts.'

'Are you having a baby?' Bethany spluttered and then went very red, as did Louise.

'Why . . .' she stammered, 'why do you ask?'

'Because you're the same shape as the mother of Amanda Callaghan who is in my class. Amanda's mother is having a baby.'

Bethany paused breathlessly, but she was beginning to regain her composure. 'I can't *quite* describe it.' She formed a balloon out of her cupped hands. 'It's . . . well something in front and a funny shape from behind. It's also the way you walk. I asked Mrs Barton but she said I shouldn't talk about such things.'

'Did you ask your father?'

'Oh, no. Nor Tina.'

'Why?'

Bethany looked a little confused as though frightened by her own boldness. 'I mean . . . if you *are* having a baby . . . is it Buddy?'

Louise ran her hand over her face and, chin in hand, looked at the ground, undecided as to what she should do.

If she denied it she would soon be made out to be a liar. On the other hand . . . well, it had to come out sooner or later. Serve Tina and Steve right for having ducked the issue for so long.

She inhaled deeply and then firmly took hold of Bethany's hand.

'I *am* having a baby,' she said, 'you're very observant. But the father isn't Buddy.' She paused

115

again, uncertain as to how to proceed. 'You see it is very complicated, but the baby inside me will be a little brother or sister for you.'

'Oh not *Daddy*. Oh I *said* Daddy should have married you, and not Tina.' And she burst into tears.

William came up to see what was going on and stood looking anxiously at his weeping sister.

'What have you done to Beth?'

'I haven't done anything to Beth.' Louise put her arm round William and drew him towards her. 'But she asked me if I was having a baby. I suppose she talked about it to you?'

William reddened and gazed at the ground.

'I told Bethany she was right. I am having a baby; but they are rather special circumstances you see.' As Bethany, overcome with curiosity, quickly dried her tears and William remained in a reluctant hug close to her, Louise went on: 'Your daddy and Tina would like to have a baby of their own, but Tina had some illness which prevented her from carrying one to full term. She could start a baby but it would come away, and she lost several at about three months or so. This made your father and Tina very unhappy.' She paused. 'Well, one day I saw a programme on the TV about women who could carry babies for couples who were unable to have their own. As I am fond of your father . . . and Tina . . . I offered to do this for them.'

'But how can you do that?' Bethany looked aghast, while William, redder than ever, had his eyes closed as his embarrassment deepened.

'Daddy's seed and an egg from Tina were fertilised outside the body in a laboratory, and when the tiny embryo was formed it was put safely

116

inside my tummy, so you see I am carrying . . .'

'But how did it get there?' Bethany's eyes were wide open with wonder.

'The doctor put it there. It is all tucked away safely now until December when it will come out and you will have a new baby brother or sister. There. Isn't that exciting?'

*   *   *

The children were very quiet on the way home, so quiet that Louise got rather anxious and wondered whether she should have told them as much as she had. After all, though seeming much older, Bethany was only twelve and how much she really knew or understood about the facts of life was hard to fathom.

Children were so much more grown-up than when she had been small, but she thought that even at twelve she had a pretty good idea of where babies came from and how they got there.

'Promise to say nothing to Daddy or Tina,' she said as she stopped the car in front of the house.

'But why not?' Bethany screwed up her eyes in a gesture of rebelliousness that Louise knew well.

'Because they want to tell you themselves as a surprise. A *nice* surprise I hope.'

'I wish you were the real mummy,' Bethany said wistfully and then, as if she couldn't trust herself any further, opening the door of the car she flew across the courtyard towards the house while William, still looking bemused, remained rooted to the spot.

'You won't . . . will you William?'

But William, too embarrassed to speak, merely

shook his head and slowly made his way after his sister.

CHAPTER EIGHT

Tina looked round Bethany's room, picked up the duvet and pillows from the floor, put them back onto the bed and made some attempt to make it. The room was a shambles; clothes on the floor, half open drawers with a medley of garments cascading from them. There were two dirty plates, and glasses sticky with congealed milk on the pretty dressing table which Tina had gone to so much trouble with when planning Bethany's room during extensive redecorations that had been done in the house the year before.

She had wanted to do her best to make Bethany feel at home, that she had her own place, her own pad; the pretty floral cretonnes and wallpaper, the attractive white custom-built furniture Tina had personally chosen with such care. The carpet had been a rich strawberry colour, the curtains matched the wallpaper and the duvet cover synchronised with the overall decorative plan.

All for what?

In the middle of the carpet was an ugly stain. It looked like blood but as far as she knew Bethany had not started her period, and if it wasn't blood it was impossible to fathom what it could be.

Tina sighed. It was very hard to be a stepmother. Lots of things were written about it but no one really seemed to know exactly what to do or how to handle children who refused to be wooed or reconciled, however hard the step-parent tried.

Even Bethany's own mother found her difficult which was some consolation.

Finishing her half-hearted attempt to tidy up, and still feeling bruised and angry, Tina went along to the bedroom where Steve was lying on the bed reading the paper. He looked up at her and smiled, patting the place beside him.

'You look cross, darling. Something wrong?'

'I've just been into Bethany's room. You never *saw* such a mess. It is an absolute pigsty and I tried so hard. Even some of the wallpaper looks as though she tried to strip it from the wall.'

'Oh, come on, darling. You're exaggerating. She would never do *that*.'

'There's a horrible stain in the middle of the floor. God knows what it is.'

In exasperation Steve changed the subject. 'I thought we'd have a short holiday abroad, Bermuda, the Seychelles, Florida. What do you fancy? Just us. No children.'

He pressed her close to him and kissed her cheek.

Tina's eyes widened. 'Are you serious? I thought you were very busy?'

'Perfectly serious. It's a good time to go. I've looked up planes and places on the Internet. I can book right away, any destination you want to go to.'

'But Steve what about the children? They've another week here. Won't they be upset if we don't take them?'

'I think you need a break away from them. I've talked to Louise. She's perfectly willing to have them.'

'Louise agreed?'

'Of course. Why not?'

'Didn't she mind?'

Steve looked surprised. 'Mind? Why should she mind? I think she quite likes the idea of being in charge. I said I'd make it up to her after the baby is born. Give us time to get to know our child and nice for her to go away. I've suggested she should go with Buddy.' Steve winked. 'Maybe he'll pop the question.'

Tina lay back on the bed and closed her eyes.

Really it all seemed too good to be true.

*   *   *

When Steve and Tina got downstairs the children were in the television room. While Steve went to book their tickets for the Seychelles on the Internet, Tina went into the kitchen to prepare dinner. Vegetables were usually left by Mrs Barton ready to cook, and sometimes there was a pie or chicken or piece of beef or lamb already in the oven.

Culinary skills were not among Tina's accomplishments. She had never really learned to cook. As a model, food did not figure high on her list of priorities, due to the necessity of always having to keep pencil slim. She had tended, then, to smoke a lot and eat little.

When she was married to Denis he managed to persuade her to give up smoking but not to learn to cook. They ate out a lot.

Steve was something of a gourmet and liked his food. Tina couldn't hope to compete with chefs from the finest restaurants. But Steve was a good cook and not above producing a meal from time to time.

Tina, meanwhile, had been having lessons from Mrs Barton and now could manage a reasonably tasty, if rudimentary, meal consisting of a first course, a main dish and a sweet. Tonight it was avocado with prawns which, already prepared and dressed by Mrs Barton, waited in the fridge, chicken casserole, already in the oven, and vegetables which only needed to be cooked.

She and Steve always had a drink before dinner in the lounge and usually the children joined them there before going in to dinner, which was early so that Bethany and William could eat with them.

Steve came in rubbing his hands just as Bethany wandered along the corridor, her normal sulky expression on her face. Steve put an arm round her and ushered her inside.

'I've got a nice surprise for you,' he said. 'You are to have Louise to yourself for a whole ten days. She's going to come and sleep up here.'

'Why?' Bethany looked suspiciously at her father. 'Where are you going?'

'I am taking Tina away for a short break. The Seychelles. I've already booked our tickets.'

Tina's heart sank. She wished Steve could have thought of a more tactful way to tell them, and she was right as immediately Bethany's face crumpled:

'But why can't *we* go?'

'Because Tina and I want a little time alone together and we know how you like being with Louise.'

'But you *said* . . .' Bethany kneaded her fists in her eyes like a baby about to cry. 'You *said* we'd go to Bermuda.'

Steve's expression was patient. 'I said we would

try but it hasn't been possible. Now, as it happens I have a short break in the building work and . . .'

'It's not *fair*.' Clearly working herself up to a tantrum Bethany stamped her foot petulantly. 'You said . . .'

'How about skiing at Christmas time?' Steve began and then looked at Tina who was anxiously shaking her head. 'Oh, no . . . maybe in January, or February . . .'

'Or not at all,' Bethany stormed. *'You're* breaking your promises, changing your mind . . .'

'I am not . . .' Steve began weakly.

'Your father did not change his mind,' Tina broke in, irritated beyond measure not only by Bethany's behaviour but by the way she could twist her father round her little finger. Any minute now Steve would rush off and book two more tickets. 'And while we're on the subject of breaking promises, Bethany, may I remind you that you promised to keep your room clean and tidy, and it is like a pigsty. I was quite shocked when I popped in to see it today. You promised me . . .'

'I did *not* promise you, you old cow,' Bethany screamed. 'And don't you dare go snooping about in my room. It is nothing to do with you.'

'On the contrary,' the colour surged to Tina's cheeks, 'it is a lot to do with me. I went to a great deal of trouble making your room look pretty and nice, and I was horrified when I saw the state it was in today. Perhaps if you kept your room nice and did as you were told your father might be more inclined to take you on holiday with us . . .'

'You just don't want me.'

'No, I don't want you, since you ask.' The colour had now drained away and Tina's face was chalky

122

white. 'Frankly I've had a ghastly time with you this summer. You seem to do all you can to make life difficult for me. You are so ungrateful. We do our very best to give you a good time . . .'

'I hate you,' Bethany spat at her. 'No wonder you can't manage a baby of your own, but have to get someone else to have it for you. You must be all screwed up and twisted inside . . .' As she spoke she contorted her body and grimaced like a gargoyle, 'all twisty and horrible.'

'Don't you dare speak to Tina like that,' Steve said sternly. 'You don't know what you're saying.'

'Oh yes I do.' Bethany gave him a knowing look. 'Louise told us all about how she offered to have a baby for you. Well I think it's perfectly disgusting, a horrible thing to do. If you can't have a baby in the normal way you should have done without. I don't want a brother or a sister who's a freak.'

'When did Louise tell you?' To her surprise Tina found she could control her emotion and manage to keep her voice very, almost deadly, calm.

'A couple of days ago.' Bethany now appeared to have run out of steam, and hung her head. 'She asked us not to say anything. Well, I'm glad she told us. I now know what sort of person you are. I was right all the time and I think Daddy made a horrible mistake marrying you. He should have married Louise as I told him.' She spun round to face her father. 'Didn't I, Daddy? Didn't I tell you you should have married Louise?'

'Would you go to your room please, Bethany?' Steve pointed sharply to the door. 'And don't come out until I tell you.'

'No I won't,' Bethany said hysterically stamping her feet again. 'I'm going to telephone Mummy

123

and ask her to come and take me home.'

'You know perfectly well that your mother isn't in the country and won't be until the end of next week.'

'Well, I shan't stay here in the same house as *her.*' She threw a venomous glance in Tina's direction. 'I shall go straightaway to Louise and ask if I can stay with her.' And turning her back on her stepmother and father she ran out of the room cannoning into William who was just entering.

'What's going on?' he asked bewilderedly as Bethany shot past him like a whirlwind, and in a few seconds there was the mighty sound of the door banging.

*   *   *

It was a very silent meal, also rather overcooked by the time it was served. So shocked by what had happened Tina hardly knew what she was doing in the kitchen. Steve, his glass replenished with a stiff measure of whisky, had stayed in the lounge to explain the situation to William.

Now William sat between them, also silent, and clearly ill at ease.

At the end of the meal they all sat gazing at their plates. Tina had scarcely touched her food.

'What's going to happen to Bethany?' William asked after a while.

'I'll go and telephone Louise,' Steve said, glad of the chance to get up. 'On second thoughts maybe I'd better go round and see her.' He put out a hand. 'Come with me William?'

He looked across at Tina who shook her head.

'I'll clear away and then I think I'll go to bed,'

she said wearily. 'Frankly I feel I've had quite enough for one day.'

*   *   *

Tina was sure she had been asleep rather than dozing when she heard the door open and Steve creep in. The lights on either side of the bed glowed softly, and she was aware of him coming over to her and standing by the side of the bed looking at her. His presence unnerved her and she opened her eyes and stared at him.

'I thought you were asleep?' he said and sat down beside her.

'I was,' she said.

'Sorry.' He bent and kissed her cheek. 'It's terribly late.' Glancing at the clock Tina saw it was after midnight.

'Where have you been all this time?' she murmured. 'With Louise?'

'Well, I had a lot of sorting out to do. At first Bethany refused to come away. In the end Louise persuaded her. She was very good.'

Tina gazed mulishly at her husband.

'Where is Bethany now?'

'Oh, in bed. I brought her back with me. Louise came too and helped to settle her down. Then, of course, I had to take her home again.'

'Of course.'

'Don't sound so sarcastic, darling. I couldn't let her walk back alone in the middle of the night.'

Tina judged it wisest not to reply.

'I think it's going to be alright with Bethany,' Steve went on. 'After we, Louise and I, had finished talking to her she began to sound quite reasonable.

She's sorry for the way she spoke to you,' he paused, 'though we shall have to postpone our holiday.'

'Again?'

'Well it's hardly the time to go away, is it, with Bethany in such a state? Louise thinks we should wait until she goes back to school.'

'It seems to me that Louise is governing our lives, not just having our baby.'

'Don't be ridiculous, Tina,' Steve said irritably getting up and beginning to pace the room. 'You really are most unreasonable about Louise. I sense every time you mention her name that you resent her.'

'That is *not* true, Steve, but she does seem to have taken over. You hang onto her every word.'

'I do not,' Steve said indignantly. 'I really resent that. I am just trying to make the best of a bad situation. We have had a most difficult summer. The complications with the building haven't helped. Sometimes I wish I'd never started the damn thing.'

'Or let Louise have our baby,' Tina added bitterly.

Steve ceased his pacing and stared at her.

'Do you really mean that?'

'Yes I do.' Tina swept her hair away from her face. 'It was a big mistake. I've never got used to it and I think deep down neither have you. Bethany's right. It *is* a freakish situation. Our baby was conceived in a test-tube and implanted in the womb of another woman from whom it gets nutrients. She can partly claim that she is its mother.' Tina let her gaze rest on Steve's troubled face. 'I've always suspected, in my heart of hearts, that Louise was in love with you and I think she wanted to be impregnated with your child. It was her way of getting you. I'm sure of it.'

'That *is* absurd,' Steve spluttered. 'Why, it's almost obscene.'

'Nevertheless I think it's true. Besides, why did she tell the children she was pregnant?' Tina demanded. 'To cause trouble. We specifically asked her not to. She must have had a reason.'

'But they asked her. Bethany asked her directly, saying she was the same shape as the pregnant mother of a school friend. Louise then explained it as best she could.'

'Huh!' Tina snorted and sank below the duvet so that it almost covered her face.

'You really *are* prejudiced against Louise.' Steve flopped onto the bed again. 'I want you to try and be sisters.'

'I don't think that's possible.'

'But she told me you once suggested it.'

'Did I?' Tina raised her head looking surprised. 'That must have been in better times.'

'Then what went wrong?'

'I can't explain it, Steve. I suppose it is simply that I don't like Louise or particularly trust her. Maybe I never did. Maybe I regarded her as a rival. After all, you knew her long before you knew me. There's a familiarity between you that I find unsettling, always have. Even Bethany says you should have married her. Perhaps she was right.'

'But Tina, darling,' Steve leaned over her and tenderly stroked her brow. 'I do *not* love Louise. I love you. I explained that to Bethany. I also told her that if Louise had been her stepmother she might not have liked her either. The fact is that she would resent anyone who took the place of Frances. I can't help that because Frances left me, as I told Bethany.'

'Oh, it seems that you've done a lot of explaining behind my back.'

Steve got up and, with a gesture of weariness, removed his jacket and hung it over the back of a chair, then he turned again and faced his wife.

'Tina, I think you have brought a lot of this on yourself. You have not been exactly fair to Louise and I think to bring that up about Bethany's room tonight just before dinner was very shortsighted, even if it is true.'

'I was trying to defend you about broken promises.'

'Nevertheless it was not the right time. Bethany is only twelve. She may try to be grown-up and know all about babies but she isn't. She is a rather confused, fragile child. I am going to have a good talk to the housemistress when I take her to her new school. Meanwhile I would like you to try and get on as best you can for the rest of the holiday, and also change your attitude to Louise. She's been a real brick.'

*   *   *

Tina finished writing the note on her bureau in the bedroom, read it through then tucked it into an envelope and hid it under her blotter in case Steve came in. That morning, neither of them had said much as they went through their ablutions and dressed. In fact, neither had had a very good night. Steve tossed and turned and Tina lay listening to him and thinking, aware of his stiff, unresponsive

128

body in the bed beside her.

By dawn her mind had been made up and she slept a little. It was perhaps not the best time to come to a crucial decision in the middle of the night, but in the cold light of day she still felt the same.

Steve had gone down to breakfast but she didn't follow him. After he had gone she quickly, almost furtively, packed a suitcase, got her passport from the locked drawer in the bureau and wrote Steve the note.

She could always come back.

She tucked everything out of sight and when she did go down it was to make sure the coast was clear. Mrs Barton was in the kitchen and called out a cheery morning greeting.

'Morning Mrs L.'

'Good morning Mrs Barton. Is my husband about?'

'I think he went off with the children, Mrs L.' Mrs Barton looked at her askance. 'Said something about the seaside as it's such a nice day. I think Louise went with them.'

'I'd better see who's in the shop,' Tina said with a worried frown.

'Oh, I saw Ruth go in.'

Tina's brow cleared. 'In that case I'll give her a ring.'

Tina had coffee and a piece of toast, chatting quite calmly to the housekeeper. Then she went back to her bedroom, completed her packing and looked around. She was helped in her decision by the fact that this was now, undoubtedly, a declaration of war.

Steve had not tried to make up with her for his

129

accusations the night before. Instead he had taken the children to the seaside, without consulting her and, in a deliberate act of provocation, had taken Louise.

She withdrew the note from under the blotter and propped it against the clock on her bureau where Steve would be sure to see it as he came through the door. After a final look round she took her suitcase, went down the back stairs to the garage and put it in the boot of her car. She threw in her coat and handbag and went round to the kitchen.

'I'm just off up to London, Mrs Barton. I may be away a few days. Take care of things in my absence will you?'

'Of course Mrs L.' Mrs Barton looked surprised. 'Is everything alright?'

Tina gazed calmly around. 'As far as I can see. I phoned Ruth and asked her to hold the fort. Please tell Mr Lockwood I shan't be here for dinner.'

*   *   *

Louise lay on her stomach letting the sand run through her fingers. The sun beat upon her back but she had protected her head with a sunhat. This was bliss. She rested her head on her hands and looked sideways at the waves rolling up onto the beach. She could just make out Steve, Bethany and William gambolling in the water, ducking under the waves as they splashed about, and laughing at one another.

Heaven. The beach at Burton Bradstock was sheltered by high cliffs on either side and, although it attracted a lot of people, there always seemed room for them. It was very much a family venue.

And she felt *they* were a family—she, Steve, Bethany and William and, of course, the baby inside her.

She turned on her back and rested her hands on her bump. It was rounding nicely. The baby moved about a lot. She was sure it was a boy. The clinic knew the sex after a recent scan, but neither she nor the baby's parents wanted to know. Buddy had again taken her, but there had been no need to stay the night. She was pronounced fit and even Janice had ceased her pep talks and sent her on her way, wishing her well.

Finally the three left the water and Bethany rushed up the beach to flop beside her.

'Isn't this *nice*?' she asked, relaxed and smiling, very different from the girl the day before.

'Lovely.' Louise put an arm round her, watching Steve walk slowly along the beach, his arm round William.

'I'm glad Tina's not here, aren't you?'

Louise screwed up her eyes.

'You must try and make it up with Tina, you know. She is your stepmother and that situation isn't going to change.'

'I hate her.'

'No, I don't really think you do. Resent her, perhaps. But as she and your father are now not going on holiday just to be with you, don't you think you should make some sort of effort to try and be nice to her?'

'No,' Bethany said unequivocally and lightly touched Louise's stomach. 'I wish the baby really *was* yours.'

'I do too,' Louise said gazing at the sky shading

131

her eyes against the sun. 'Sometimes I feel it is. I think about it a lot. After all, I have not exactly given it life, but I have allowed it to grow. I feed it. Without me it could not develop.' She lowered her gaze to look at Bethany. 'You mustn't think it's a freak. It's not.'

Bethany hung her head.

'I only said that to annoy Tina.'

'Well, you succeeded. You annoyed your father too. I did ask you to say nothing, then none of this would have happened.'

'Oh yes it would,' Bethany said, her voice loaded with spite. 'It was all going to come out. They should have told us a long time ago and not made such a secret of it. It's their fault not yours.' She tucked her hand trustfully into that of Louise's and gazed at her adoringly. 'I do *wish* you were my mummy.'

Louise looked past the head of the young girl and saw that Steve was standing close to them. He must have heard what his daughter had said.

'Did you have a nice time?' she asked quickly.

'Lovely.' Steve sat down and started to dry himself. The salty sea water glistened on his body and his hair was wet and crumpled. She thought he looked magnificent. His torso was sinewy with strong pectoral muscles and a mat of fine fair hair covering his chest.

At that moment Louise felt an immense physical longing for him. She could imagine their bodies entwined and with that came a rush of despair that they never would be, and that this was as close, probably, as they would ever get.

It wasn't fair. It wasn't right.

'Like an ice cream?' Steve finished drying

132

himself, unaware of the turmoil in his companion's breast. 'Then I think we should get back. I tell you what, we'll pick up Tina and all go out to dinner.'

'That would be lovely,' Louise murmured wishing he hadn't thought it necessary to include Tina. But of course he did it because he thought he should. He had told her a little about the night before and how angry Tina had been. She made him feel guilty. Surely he realised that the four of them as they were now made a perfect family and didn't need anyone else?

Steve felt in his beach bag for his mobile phone and punched in the number. 'I feel bad about Tina,' he said as he put it to his ear. 'I should have tried to make up with her before I left this morning. I should have asked her to come with us.'

Of course you should, Louise thought looking at him askance. Only you didn't. Why? Because you wanted to be alone with me and the children. Why not face up to it Steve?

Steve let the telephone ring for a few seconds then turned it off and tucked it away in his beach bag.

'No reply,' he said, 'she must be in the shop. I'll try again later.'

*   *   *

It was a happy, noisy trip home. The children, having managed to get their father to cancel, or at least postpone his holiday until they were back at school, were in good spirits, and for Louise sitting beside Steve it had been a perfect day.

They had rung the shop to be told by Ruth that Tina hadn't appeared all day. This made Steve feel

133

even more uncomfortable.

'I hope this hasn't brought on one of her migraine attacks,' he said. 'She's been so much better lately. I think I've been thoughtless.'

As soon as he stopped the car in front of the house he leapt out only pausing to tell them to go and have a wash, get ready and meet again in half an hour.

'I need to change,' Louise protested. Knowing she wouldn't swim she had kept on the clothes she had put on when she got up.

'No you don't. You look fine. Keep an eye on the children for me.'

'Of course, Steve.' Louise smiled and after collecting all their things they followed Steve into the house.

Steve climbed the stairs two at a time, conscious of a nagging fear that all was not well with Tina. He had behaved very stupidly, very impulsively and now wished that he'd had the good sense to try and make up in the morning. They usually did after any tiff they might have, and they were not all that uncommon.

But he had felt very angry. Now, after a good relaxing day in the sun with the children on their best behaviour, that anger had gone and he only wished they'd brought Tina with them to share it. The sun and the sea would have helped to relax her too.

He opened the bedroom door and looked round, seeing the white envelope propped up on the bureau opposite immediately. His heart froze over completely as he picked it up and tore it open.

Steve, (it said in Tina's rounded scrawl)

I felt I should get away for a while, a few days, a week or so. I don't know. I might stay longer until the children have gone to school. I might even go for ever. I just don't know now how I really feel.

My relationship with Bethany at the moment is disastrous and I don't know what to do about it. You and I don't seem to understand each other. I think it's best for all of us that we try and sort something out, think this thing through which we don't seem able to do when we are together.

I think I'll go to Paris and look at the fashions. They always cheer me up. But I'll be in touch.

The children anyway will be happier without me. I've handled Bethany badly, I realise that. Maybe I haven't got it in me to be a good mother.

Have a nice time.

I love you Steve.

Tina.

CHAPTER NINE

The rain had made it difficult to proceed with the building. Only the foundations had been laid. But even when it stopped the workmen managed to be elsewhere and Steve had reached a point where his patience was finally beginning to snap. The trouble with using self-employed men was that they always had a good excuse for being somewhere else. There were days when even the work's supervisor was nowhere to be seen, like today. The site was empty.

During the wet weather they always found jobs to do inside and these they wanted to complete and be paid for before they would come out again.

Steve, wearing his protective helmet, shoulders hunched, hands deep in the pockets of his duffel coat, made his way round the foundations and stared gloomily into the pit which was still half full of water. It would take days to drain. Already some of the bricks had arrived to start the building and stood in desolate piles half hidden under tarpaulin. Heaven knew when the job would be completed. It was weeks behind schedule and everyone blamed someone else, or they all conspired to blame the weather.

Steve looked around at the chaos of the site: the mud, the mixers, patches of hardened cement and all the flotsam and jetsam of the building trade. It was a depressing business. He should have employed a decent, responsible firm of contract builders and not tried to cut corners by relying on self-employed workmen who, however excellent, in turn employed other casual labour by the hour or the day.

There was a step behind him and he looked around to see Louise gazing at him sympathetically. His heart sank. Louise always seemed to hover, to know where he was and try and deduce how he was feeling as if in an effort to replace Tina who had still not returned home, though he knew she was in Paris.

Louise meant well but seemed unable to realise she was an added irritation rather than a comfort.

'Didn't any of them turn up today?' she asked.

Steve gazed at the cloud-laden sky.

'They thought it might rain. The longer I have

this hole in the ground the more interest I'm having to pay to the bank. Sometimes I wish I'd never started.'

'Oh Steve,' impulsively Louise tucked a hand through his resisting arm. 'You mustn't say that. It's a wonderful scheme and you see, by Easter . . .' she stopped.

By Easter who knew what would happen?

He looked at her as if he could read her thoughts. 'Things haven't gone well have they?' he said at last. 'Tina doing a bunk, the building practically coming to a halt. It wasn't a particularly good year in the shop.'

'But we made a profit!' Louise said cheerfully. She always tried to be robust and optimistic when she was with Steve because lately he had been so down in the mouth.

'Just about,' he mumbled.

'Oh, Steve,' impatiently Louise withdrew her hand. 'You *won't* be cheered up. You must *want* to be miserable.'

'No I don't.' Steve leaned against a pile of bricks. 'I am naturally an optimistic person, but you must face realities. It was no situation for you in which to have to bear somebody else's child. But seven months ago it didn't seem like that. Seven months is a very long time.'

'I don't regret it,' Louise said, staring at him defiantly.

'Not one little bit?' He put his head on one side.

'Not a tiny little bit.' She paused and went on, 'I only wish the baby was mine.' She put her hands gingerly on her stomach. 'I feel it *is* mine. I feel such a bond with it and, Steve . . . if Tina doesn't come back . . .'

137

'Yes?' Steve waited for her to finish with a sense of dread.

'Well . . . maybe we could bring the baby up together?'

* * *

Yes, Tina hadn't fully thought that out had she? Steve thought savagely as he trudged back to the house after leaving Louise at the shop where she was now in sole charge, Ruth having taken up her place at university. She hadn't considered what would happen to Louise expecting their baby, or to him now in a highly compromising position. Although a few people knew the truth most didn't and had drawn their own conclusions, that is that Tina had gone away after finding out that Louise and her husband were having an affair.

What else were they meant to think? And Louise played on this for all she was worth.

Sometimes, now, Steve dreaded seeing Louise alone, whereas before he had always enjoyed her company because he didn't regard her as a threat. But in the past few weeks since Tina had left she had somehow turned threatening, there was no doubt about it. She was like his shadow, keeping an eye on him and whenever he found himself alone there was Louise at his side, or close by, offering comfort, advice, desperately keen on being unobtrusive yet always seeming to intrude.

Maybe it was her predicament that made him feel guilty? It didn't seem fair, but all he knew was that the more he saw Louise the less he wanted to see her, that he desperately missed his wife and wished she would come back.

138

Tina had written from Paris to try and explain more fully what had happened. It wasn't just the row with Bethany, his reaction and lack of sympathy. The fundamental reason for her flight she realised was Louise. She bitterly regretted letting Louise have their baby. It has been a mad idea, Louise had become an intrusion in their lives and she found she had come to dislike her. She thought they had got themselves into an impossible situation and didn't know how they were going to get out of it.

She felt Louise had a crush on him and he refused to acknowledge it, or admit it existed. In her view Louise threatened to take over their lives.

What, for instance, would happen when the baby was born? Were the three of them going to bring it up? Louise would always feel she had proprietorial rights to a child who, after all, she had carried, nurtured. How foolish of them even to have thought otherwise? In fact, she scarcely felt now that the child was hers.

Steve had replied to the *poste restante* address begging her to give them the chance to meet and talk but she hadn't replied. The thought of having the child with Louise was anathema to him and he now, somewhat irrationally, blamed Louise for the disastrous events that had occurred in the summer, the persecution of Tina by the children that led to her flight. He even blamed Louise for the effects of the weather on the building programme while knowing that was unfair too.

Steve arrived at the back door of the house, took off his muddy wellington boots and his coat and hat and shook them before entering the kitchen where he found Mrs Barton, her stout figure the

139

embodiment of calm and reassurance, stirring something that smelled delicious on the Aga. She turned as he came in.

'Any sign of the men, Mr L?'

'None at all,' Steve shook his head and collapsed on one of the chairs by the kitchen table. 'Sometimes I regret the whole project . . .'

'You mustn't do that,' Mrs Barton pushed a mug of coffee towards him. 'It will be fine when it's done.'

'But will it?' Steve said dejectedly. 'I'm not sure now that I haven't been too ambitious, and it really hasn't got the local support I had hoped for.'

There had been letters in the local press, and the council had been accused of flattery and favouritism. Now it had agreed to stop the road leading to Nether Poynton being widened for the increase in traffic that was expected, so there would be traffic jams and hold-ups for miles if the expected crowds materialised.

'Louise was in here looking for you,' Mrs Barton said in a voice without any kind of inflection.

'She found me,' Steve sighed. 'She always does.'

He looked up at Mrs Barton who cocked her head on one side.

'You know the truth, of course, don't you?' He kept his eyes on her as he drained his coffee.

'I'm not sure.' Mrs Barton brought her own mug over to the table and sat facing Steve. 'A lot of tongues are wagging.'

'The truth is that the child Louise is carrying is mine and Tina's. Tina wasn't able to bear a child and Louise offered to be a surrogate mother. I'm not at all sure that was a good idea now,' he finished almost to himself.

'Whatever is said, most people think it's your baby, Louise being so keen on you. Buddy has given them the idea.'

'Buddy knows the truth, but for some reason prefers to distort it.'

'He's very bitter.'

'I know. Oh God,' Steve buried his face in his hands. 'I wish the whole thing had never happened. I really do. As for Louise being keen on me . . . how was *I* to know?'

'I would have thought it was obvious, Mr L,' Mrs Barton said sharply. 'If you didn't realise it you must have been the only one. I'm sure your wife did.'

'I liked her as a friend, nothing more. I never gave her *any* reason to think anything else.'

'If you ask me I think you ought to try and see your wife and talk to her,' Mrs Barton said, taking her mug to the sink and rinsing it. 'I hope I don't speak out of turn but it seems to me that all you adults have behaved very foolishly, and some sense has got to come out of this situation because another person is involved.' She looked at him over her shoulder, 'You've got to think of the baby. The poor wee creature didn't ask to be born.'

*   *   *

Louise looked round the shop and felt happy, deliriously so. Once more she was stock-taking and she recalled the year before when at about the same time she had learned Tina's predicament, and slowly the idea had developed in her mind of having their baby. She supposed, if she was being honest, that at the time she had hoped the baby

141

would be hers and Steve's and this would give her a real lever over him. She had not then realised that Tina was capable of producing an egg which could be fertilised by Steve's sperm; but by the time she learned this sickening fact it was too late to go back. The idea of carrying Steve's child had been attractive, and still was. If only the other half had been hers. The irony was that Tina seemingly had now left home, which was the realisation of a dream that even Louise hadn't expected, couldn't possibly have anticipated. Now she had Steve all to herself and only two months before the baby was born.

Still time to make plans.

Looking at the merchandise she hummed a little tune. Time too to get rid of all the expensive stock Tina had insisted on buying and introduce more popular lines which she knew would sell well. Montacute and the other local stately homes just about got it right. Poynton had been way out, lucky to have survived, and now she was going to mark down all the porcelain and fancy stuff and get rid of it in the Christmas sale when lots of people came to buy little orange trees and poinsettias, and they did a nice line in Christmas tree decorations and gift-wrapped knick-knacks.

Ruth had promised to come back for the holiday just about when she was expecting the baby; but still, staffing was a worry. It had always been assumed that Tina would be there, now she sincerely hoped that she wouldn't.

Nothing, no little doubts or worries about the future could banish the joy Louise felt at being alone with Steve and the chance it gave to develop the relationship, even though he was grumpy,

142

erratic and moody; seemed at times to recoil from her presence. But it was all quite understandable, and by understanding him she knew she could bring him out and, ultimately, make him happy. It was just a matter of time. Things had happened so fast. Tina's abrupt departure and the realisation that she might not come back was a shock; but when its significance really dawned on her she could hardly contain her euphoria. It was almost as though she had a good fairy taking care of her.

Without Tina, Steve would be hers, must be. She would be patient and loving, be there when he needed her, make no demands on him, be self-effacing if necessary, and in time he would come round.

She felt she understood Steve better than he understood himself. She was sorry she'd been impatient with him just now on the building site by implying that he liked being miserable. She must show more patience and then there would be no need for him to be irritated with her, which he clearly had been.

The morning seemed to pass slowly. There were a few customers buying bulbs for spring flowering and already Louise had put some Christmas cards on display, and these were selling fast. It was wonderful to feel in control, as if she owned the place . . . which, she looked round with an air of satisfaction, one day she might if she and Steve ultimately got together and she became the third Mrs Lockwood.

Louise's face suddenly clouded. But what if Tina were to come back? Perish the thought. She shook her head, determined to banish the idea completely.

A crowd of people came in through the door and among them she spotted a familiar face, Dorothy O'Brien. She hadn't seen her since the meeting in Yeovil the year before. She waved at her and Dorothy detached herself from the crowd who had started to mill round the displays and with a look of bewilderment on her face came across to Louise.

'Hi!'

'Hi!' They kissed briefly and then Dorothy stood back and gazed at her.

'I didn't know you were . . . oh, Louise, I'm so *pleased* for you.'

'Thanks,' Louise said, attempting a shy smile.

'We should have been in touch. I know I said I'd ask you and Buddy for a meal but it has been a difficult year . . .'

'Don't worry', Louise briefly touched her arm. 'For me too. Come and have a coffee,' and she stuck a notice saying 'Back in ten minutes' in front of the till and steered her friend into the café where Susan was beginning to serve lunches.

'I'm looking round for Christmas presents,' Dorothy said distractedly. 'It's such a chore.'

As the two women sat down she leaned on the table, arms crossed. 'Well, how are you and when is it due?'

'December,' Louise replied.

'You'll be pleased.' Dorothy, Louise saw, was looking at her hand. 'Not married?'

Louise shook her head. 'Not yet, but it's not necessary these days is it?'

'Is Buddy pleased?'

'Not particularly,' Louise smiled enigmatically. 'It's not his baby.'

'Oh!'

144

Susan came over with two cups of coffee and chatted for a moment with Dorothy whom she vaguely knew. Then, after she'd left, Dorothy whispered, 'Tell me.'

'Can't you guess?' The shy smile played again on Louise's lips.

'Not Steve!' Dorothy exclaimed.

'You thought I was fantasising just because he had a glamorous, ex-model wife? Well, she left him.'

'And are you getting married?'

'Oh, I expect so. Some time. There's no hurry. The main thing is to know that Steve loves me, and he does.'

'Well I don't know.' Dorothy sat back. 'I mean . . .' words seemed to fail her.

'You told me I should see a psychiatrist,' Louise added.

Dorothy blushed.

'I know . . . I mean . . .'

'Never mind, it's not important now.' Louise studied the face of the woman opposite her. 'You said it had been a bad year?'

'I lost the baby I was expecting . . .'

'Oh, I'm sorry.'

'I didn't really want it.' Dorothy was suddenly subdued. 'But then I did after it had gone and I became depressed. And then a few months later Sean, who didn't understand, told me he was in love with someone else. So now I'm on my own. That's why I didn't get back to you.'

Louise put a hand on Dorothy's arm. 'I'm so sorry . . . and the children?'

'Oh, I have them. Sean doesn't live too far away with his new partner and he sees them. They're both at school now which is why I could have this day out, with the Women's Institute,' she sounded apologetic. 'Never thought I would. I mean, I thought I wasn't the type . . . but they are supportive. It gives me something to do.'

'Look,' Louise said suddenly, 'we badly need help in the shop. It was run by me and Steve's wife Tina. But since she left it's been hard work. We had a student in the summer and she will come back for the Christmas vacation but that is when my baby is due. Is it something that might appeal to you? Flexible hours?'

'Well,' Dorothy gazed at her nonplussed. 'It *does* sound attractive, but I'm not sure. Can I think about it?'

'Of course.' Louise glanced at the clock on the wall. 'My ten minutes was up long ago. Come and have a chat with me if you want before you leave and I'll tell you what's involved.'

*　　*　　*

The weather showed little improvement over the next few days; the pool in the pit made by the foundations seemed to get deeper. Steve sacked the supervisor and tried to engage a firm of builders to take over the work. But they were up to their eyes and couldn't give him a time when they could start, never mind finish.

He began looking further afield, met the same response and would arrive back depressed and exhausted.

After garaging his car he came in through the back entrance after one such depressing day and found the lights on in the kitchen, the table set for two and Louise standing at the bench mixing something in a bowl.

'Vinaigrette,' she said, turning to Steve with a smile. 'I thought we'd have a steak and salad, like in the old days.'

Steve forced a smile.

'That's very kind.'

'Let me take your coat,' Louise said soothingly and began to help him out of it.

'I can manage.' Steve irritably shrugged her off and then added a grudging, 'Thank you.'

Inwardly Louise acknowledged the reprimand. If she wanted to get his trust, and ultimately his love, she knew she mustn't be overprotective. She mustn't be demanding or possessive. She had told herself this so many times, over and over again. He would gradually come to realise how much she meant to him, how important she was in his life. But for the moment his mind was on Tina who had humiliated him.

She didn't mind. She still had that intense sense of euphoria whenever she was with Steve, no matter what his mood.

So she left him wriggling out of his coat and, returning to the bench poured whisky in a glass, adding soda and ice.

'I thought you'd like a drink,' she said handing it to him.

'Thanks.' He took the glass and tossed the contents back in a gulp. The liquid surged through his body, nearly choking him and he coughed, tears coming into his eyes as he looked at Louise. 'Sorry, went down the wrong way.'

She took the glass from him and refilled it.

'How was your day?' she asked casually. 'Any

luck?'

'No one thinks things will improve until after Christmas. I might as well leave it until then. I've handled the whole thing badly and I've lost a lot of money. I'm afraid my business acumen seems to have deserted me.' He didn't add 'due to too many worries'.

'I'm sure it hasn't. It's a bad time. Now, why don't you get us a nice bottle of wine from your cellar?' Louise handed him his glass. 'I shall just have a taste. It gives me heartburn.'

Louise went slowly back to the bench to finish mixing the vinaigrette. She was very heavy and her gait was slow and ponderous. She looked weary, and there were dark lines under her eyes. Steve watched her, consumed, as usual, by feelings that were a mixture of pity, guilt and a sort of despair. In fact he'd hardly noticed her for days, maybe weeks, so busy was he with thoughts of Tina, the business and the future, as if they were all mixed up together in his mind.

Yet Tina was right: Louise's pregnancy was unnatural. They had been wrong, but now, as Mrs Barton had said, they were all landed with an awesome responsibility: a fourth person was in the making who had never asked to be conceived in a laboratory dish and borne by a stranger.

Louise glanced at him, puzzled by his expression. 'It's not as bad as all that,' she said.

Steve looked up guiltily thinking that she was capable of reading his thoughts.

Louise continued, 'I mean—as you say—the whole thing will resolve itself after Christmas and by spring you'll have forgotten all about this bad time. Now, why don't you go to the cellar and get the wine?' She tossed him the keys and started peppering two large steaks that lay flattened on a board.

Steve went down into the cellar, selected a fairly young claret and put it carefully on its side in a basket. He took it upstairs and onto the table where he began drawing the cork, watched by Louise.

'Does it make a difference? All that fuss?'

'I think so.' Steve withdrew the cork and put it to his nose. Then he poured a little of the wine into the glass, sniffed it and drank.

'Quite good,' he said, 'but not warm enough.' He looked up with a more relaxed smile. 'After you've cooked the steaks it will taste better.'

Louise finished tossing the salad, sliced up some tomatoes and sprinkled them with chopped-up chives and parsley, sprinkled more of the vinaigrette over them and then carefully put the steaks into a pan containing a mixture of butter and oil.

She was certainly very capable. Mellowed a little by the effects of the drink, whisky glass in hand, Steve sat back watching her. She was capable and good natured, very good-hearted. It would be hard to fault Louise, and up to now he never had. She had never complained or moaned all the time she'd been pregnant. She'd carried on working in the shop, harder than ever since Tina's departure, asked for no special attention and, except for the blip at the beginning, the pregnancy had gone well.

But how did she really feel?

She put the steaks on the plates and the plates on the table, smiled as she took off her apron and sat down, her face slightly flushed from the warmth

149

of the cooker.

'How do you *really* feel?' he asked. 'You know, now, about the baby?'

'As I always did.' Louise reached for the mustard and put a dollop on the side of her plate. 'Strange how I yearn for strong flavours.' She passed him the mustard. 'Why? How do *you* feel?'

Steve didn't reply but poured a little more wine into his glass and tasted that. 'Better,' he said adding more wine and then pouring some into a glass which he pushed over to her. 'I mean the wine tastes better.' He leaned back swirling it round in its glass. 'How do I feel? Confused frankly.'

'Confused about what? The situation? Tina?'

'Yes. Both. I want Tina back here where she belongs. I want our baby when it's born to have a mother and a father. Whatever you say or feel, Louise, it is not your child and Tina has behaved very badly in shying away from her responsibilities. Nevertheless, I love her and she belongs here.'

'I see.' Louise lowered her head and for some time her gaze rested on the table, but her mind was calculating wildly. 'Then why don't you go and see her? Have it out with her?'

'Because I don't know where she's staying in Paris. If I did I'd be there like a shot. I only have a *poste restante* address and I've written twice but she doesn't reply.'

'If you ask me,' Louise cut carefully into the thick slice of entrecote, 'she wants out. What will you do then, Steve?'

'I can't think.' Steve took a large gulp of wine. 'My mind refuses to accept such a situation. Bringing up a child she wanted by myself is something I didn't bargain for.'

Louise's gaze rested for some time on him. 'But it needn't be by yourself. You'll have me. I know it's not the same, but I'll do what I can to fit in with your life. I promise I won't be obtrusive. I just want to be helpful, because . . .' she paused and swallowed hard, 'because I'm very fond of you . . .' she paused again and her expression was vulnerable and appealing, 'as I think you are of me.'

'Of course I'm fond of you,' Steve said. 'And I appreciate enormously what you've done. But I can't see how we can share bringing up the baby together, that is if we have to.'

'Then what will you do?' Her tone became shrill. 'Have it adopted? If so . . .'

'Of course I wouldn't have it adopted . . .'

'Because,' Louise went on heatedly, 'if that is what you want, if you wanted out, I would like to adopt it . . .'

'I do *not* want to have it adopted.' Steve's voice also rose. 'Is that clear? I feel in my bones that Tina will see sense and come back . . .'

'Whatever happens, Steve,' Louise had now managed to regain control of her emotions, 'I don't want to be the cause of any distress. It is your baby and I do not renege on my promise. Anything I can do to help I will . . .'

Steve felt a sudden unexpected rush of tenderness for the woman sitting opposite him who, somehow, had been sucked into a situation that was not entirely of her own making. They, after all, had concurred. He had been rather brutal with her. Had she not done what she had for them, maybe specifically for him? He now regretted repaying her kindness and goodwill with his suspicious thoughts, bad temper, unconfirmed assumptions made on the insinuation of others: that she was in love with him or, at least, had a crush on him.

Impulsively he reached over and took her hand. 'You really are a brick,' he said.

At the pressure of his hand tears came into Louise's eyes, and she quickly brushed them away as if she was ashamed of herself.

'Sorry,' she said, 'going all gooey and emotional; but I do value your support and friendship. It means a lot to me . . . and Steve I wonder if, until the baby is born, I could move in here? You know, into the house? I do feel a little nervous and afraid on my own now that the time is so close. Supposing something happened in the middle of the night? I'd feel much safer here knowing you were near. You know,' she looked at him with her large appealing eyes brimming over with emotion, 'Tina *did* once suggest it and after all I think she was right.'

CHAPTER TEN

Tina looked round the small stuffy apartment near the Gare du Nord. It was not a salubrious part of Paris and the last place she would have chosen, had she the means. The Left Bank, Avenue Foch or Saint Germain, would have been much preferred quarters.

The problem was that, although she was married to a rich man, she was not a wealthy woman in her own right. She had a generous allowance from Steve but no money of her own, and as that allowance came from an English bank it would be hard to access it once she had got through what she had, and that had nearly all gone on an expensive hotel, the sort of place she liked and was used to. Steve, she was sure, was not a vindictive man but he could easily put a stop to her allowance in an effort to force her to talk to him, and as yet she did not feel ready for it.

Her companion looked out of the window onto the grimy scene and frowned. 'You can't live here,' he said.

'It's not bad.' Tina looked around. It was small but clean and the furniture was tolerable. It had a bedroom, living room, small kitchen and bathroom with a toilet. It was also on the top floor, though up a steep flight of stairs, so on a good day it would be light and the windows could be opened to let in the air.

Still, she felt downcast, oppressed. The whole quarter was depressing, with the noise of trains entering and leaving the busy station like a distant rumble of thunder.

She had been staying at a hotel on the Avenue Montaigne and the money would soon run out.

'Let's go and think about it,' she said, but her voice lacked enthusiasm and Pierre de Marly knew that Tina would never live in a place like this.

They walked slowly down the numerous stairs and it was a relief to get out onto the street again, even though it was a wet oppressive day with grey, overcast skies. Pierre tucked his arm through hers and smiled.

'Cheer up,' he said, 'we'll think of something,' and hailing a taxi he directed it to the Place Vendôme where he had his own luxurious apartment near to the Ritz Hotel. In the taxi he put his arm round her and pressed her close. Tina shut her eyes and leaned her head against the back seat.

Pierre was an ex-boyfriend from her modelling days. He was much older than she was and he had been married then (and was now), but it had not stopped them having a passionate affair. Since then they had only vaguely kept in touch, a Christmas card, the odd phone call. He'd congratulated her on both of her marriages but she hadn't seen him since.

He was the sort of man who was a friend as well as a lover, someone with whom you could feel relaxed and at ease.

She'd phoned him as soon as she arrived in Paris and he came round at once and, as in the old days, escorted her to galleries and fashion shows, nice places to lunch or dine. He seemed to be trying to woo her all over again, but subtly as though he had all the time in the world—or perhaps another mistress as well. She didn't ask but it would be unlike Pierre to be unattached.

She was a woman who needed a man and it made her vulnerable. It was a weakness. Pierre's wife lived in the country and Tina had never met her. He had grown-up children, all married. He was a grandfather several times over. In a way he reminded her of Denis, but whereas Denis had had other women, here she was the other woman, cast in a role she both deplored and despised.

At the time when she was younger and unmarried it had not seemed too bad—everyone knew Frenchmen had mistresses—but now it was out of the question. Pierre was just a friend, a good old friend. In fact he was nearly sixty but well

154

preserved and, she had no doubt, still virile.

As if to prove it he leapt athletically out of the taxi and after helping her out, paid and steered her in the direction of his apartment. They took the lift to the second floor, to a carpeted hall, satin wallpaper with good prints on the walls, and a sturdy white-painted front door with brass fittings. He let them in and helped her off with her coat.

Tina wandered into the main salon rubbing her hands.

'Cold?' Pierre asked solicitously. 'I'll turn up the heating.'

'It's not necessary,' she said turning to him with a smile. She had on a white cashmere jumper suit with a pink scarf tucked in the neck and wore high-heeled matt black boots. Her cheeks were pink with cold and she anxiously fluffed out her hair in front of the Louis XV ormolu mirror. Pierre stood behind her and put both hands on her shoulders, leaned his face against hers.

'You look very lovely,' he said softly. 'Very desirable. Do you know you've hardly changed at all?'

'Oh, come on, Pierre,' Tina said, laughing. 'That was many years ago.'

'In fact, I think you look better than ever.' Pierre, well-practised in the art of seduction, and in no hurry, moved away and took a cigarette from an onyx cigarette box, lit it with a heavy silver lighter. 'You don't any more do you?' he asked offering her the box.

Tina shook her head, sat down on the sofa and crossed her legs. 'I wish I knew what to do.'

'Well, you can't take that apartment. No one would ever come and visit you there.'

155

She shook her head. 'Pierre, I haven't any of my own money. I have a very good allowance, but Steve could stop it any time he wanted. Probably already has.'

'But he's not a spiteful man is he?'

'Not at all. But he is very upset. You can hardly blame him. I've got us all into a terrible predicament. But I feel I don't want that child. I really don't. It's not mine.'

Pierre stood in front of the fireplace drawing thoughtfully on his cigarette. 'That's certainly a problem,' he said.

'The whole thing is a disaster.' Tina put her head in her hands. 'Do you know the baby is due in a month? But I just felt I couldn't stand any more of it, her, Louise that is, Steve, Steve's awful children. I felt my brain would explode inside my head. I had to get away and now I am afraid to go back.'

'But why?' he asked softly.

'Because the moment is past. I have left it too long. I should have stayed away just a few days, no longer than a week. Now I feel I can't face him. He must hate me, despise me. As for that woman . . . she is probably in her seventh heaven alone with the one she adores.'

Pierre came over and sat beside her.

'Yes, I must say it is not an easy situation. Something I can hardly contemplate, but there it is,' he shook his head. 'It happens. It is a very strange world we live in. Sometimes I think doctors have exceeded their powers.'

He placed his hand over hers.

'And you and I . . . do you think we'd have a chance?'

'You want to resume where we left off?'

156

'Of course. Don't you?'

He was a handsome man, tall, well-built with thinning, grey hair. He bore a vague resemblance to the French president, Chirac, and had almost an equal amount of glamour and charm. He could have passed for forty-five and, indeed, in many ways Steve looked older. Steve's hair had much more grey in it and his face was more wrinkled, but perhaps he had had more worries than Pierre who was of the old French nobility and had inherited a vast fortune on the death of his father even though, according to French law, he had had to share it with a brother and a sister.

Yet Pierre had worked as a diplomat, a member of the staff at the Quai d'Orsay which was how she had met him during an Anglo-French fashion week.

It had been a wonderful affair for a young woman, and she had learned much from Pierre and not only about sex. He was a gourmet, knew as much about wine as Steve and enjoyed a sybaritic lifestyle. There had been parties, trips to the theatre and the opera. She returned frequently to Paris at weekends and they spent holidays in the Algarve or Tunisia. Then she met Denis and it was all over.

Through her reverie she heard Pierre saying, 'A penny for them?'

'I was thinking about the old days when we met; but you know I don't believe you can ever go back, revisit the past, in the same way. Besides, I am in love with Steve.'

'And I am in love with Chantal,' he said smoothly, referring to his wife of thirty years.

Tina laughed.

'I don't *quite* believe that!'

157

'But I *do* love her,' he insisted, 'and I don't mind if you love Steve because I am sure that one day you will go back to him.'

'If he'll have me,' she murmured.

'Oh, he'll have you,' Pierre's lips gently nuzzled her ear. 'He would be mad not to.'

'What do we do about the baby?'

Pierre shrugged.

'Tell the woman to go and live somewhere else. Give her some money. Everyone has a price . . . and this time it will probably be a high one for the foolish way in which you and Steve behaved. Now, what do you say,' he gently squeezed her arm again, 'to a little love-making?'

Tina withdrew her hand from beneath his, rose, pulled her jersey down over her skirt, picked up her handbag and looked at the door.

'I won't give up trying.' Pierre gave an exaggerated shrug. 'And you know, providing you would allow me, I think I could find you a much nicer apartment than the one we saw today, in a much better location . . . and if you would let me take care of the rent I would consider it an honour.' He put his head on one side, but as Tina failed to respond he said briskly, and in quite a different tone of voice, 'Now, let me call you a cab to take you back to the hotel.'

'No thanks, I prefer to walk.'

Pierre looked surprised.

'On a day like this?'

'I need some air.'

After he had helped her on with her coat she took his hand, pressed it and put her lips to his cheek.

'I hope you didn't take offence,' he said holding

onto her hand.

'Not at all,' she whispered back. 'But you see, I need time to think.'

Pierre took her down in the lift, kissed her hand and then chastely on the cheek as they said goodbye, and as she went off in the direction of the rue du Faubourg St Honore he stood for a while looking after her then shook his head and went back inside.

*   *   *

Tina walked briskly through the Tuileries Gardens in the direction of the Place de la Concorde and then dropped down to the Embankment and walked along by the river. Paris in any season had its charm. In winter it was somehow special. It was a city she loved and would like to have lived in.

In fact, she thought she preferred the city to the country, especially now after the year they'd had at Poynton it seemed to have lost its charm.

The manor was a lovely house and in a very attractive part of the country but its appeal had waned since . . . well, since the events of the past year. It was true she was not terribly interested in gardening and maybe some of the merchandise she had bought for the shop was, as Louise had said, way out, too sophisticated. Perhaps she was substituting in her imagination a boutique in Knightsbridge for the Rue de Rivoli, and her buying policy was all wrong. The fact is she was not really all that interested. With Steve away so much it had just been something to do. She also thought that was why she had brooded about having children.

But the deterioration in her love affair with the countryside she thought really was because of Louise and the effect she had on them; on Tina especially, as Steve seemed oblivious to Louise's interest in him, or at least said he was.

Tina had never really thought of Louise as a rival, considering that she was not Steve's type. She was not in the least glamorous or exciting, a rather pleasant, earthy, capable girl, certainly lively and intelligent, but not one to fire the blood of a man as passionate, as appreciative of female beauty, as Steve.

How little she knew. Even now she didn't know the truth, whether he even fancied Louise or whether they'd slept together. Was he the innocent he seemed? Was she the scheming and conniving bitch Tina now had firmly fixed in her mind, or had she gravely misunderstood her? Was Louise as nice, as uncomplicated, as kind and concerned as she wanted everyone to think she was?

You had to be pretty complex, even slightly deranged in Tina's opinion, to want to bear someone else's child. Rightly or wrongly Tina now felt convinced about this.

But above all she felt she had to blame herself for the folly of even thinking of allowing Louise to carry her child.

The sun appeared above the clouds, casting a pale wintry sheen on the wet Paris streets. Nevertheless there was a chill wind, and people hurried by, their heads bent, clutching their coats tightly around them.

Tina paused for a moment gazing into the less than tranquil waters of the river flecked with angry little waves caused by the strong breeze.

She felt that she was at a watershed in her life: whether to stay or whether to return.

The keen wind cut into her face and she started walking briskly again. Yes, she loved Paris. She felt at home here. She loved the wide boulevards, the shops, the varied and wonderful restaurants, the *hôtels particuliers*, town houses of the rich, many of them now turned into apartments, the plethora of monuments and old buildings, the opera and the theatre, even though her French was rudimentary. There was an élan about the place that to her mind London lacked. There was so much history in Paris, a sense of continuity, that it crowded in upon you in a way it never did in London with all its crass and badly planned modern developments. Paris had a cohesion that London completely lacked, mostly because of greed on the part of the builders and lack of foresight on the part of the planners.

Above all, for a woman who had modelled for some of the most famous couture houses there was style, a unique style possessed by no other city in the world.

But what would she do here, ensconced in a flat, the mistress of a rich man? She would be entirely dependent on Pierre for everything. He would be generous but would she be able to call her soul her own? She would be a kept woman in every sense of the word. She was kept now, but the man was her husband, and there was a difference, not only a legal one, between husband and lover. A married woman had rights. Even in this modern age a mistress hardly had any, and if she felt wronged and tried to assert them the result might be an expense she couldn't afford and publicity she would hate. Tina was sure that with Pierre it would never

161

come to anything like that. But how did she know? She had thought she knew Steve; now it seemed she hadn't really known him at all.

Tina loved luxury. She loved clothes and fine food and wine, eating in good restaurants; but would she not be Pierre's plaything, always at his beck and call? Then how long would it last? In three years' time she would be nearly forty. What if he discarded her; what if he already had a younger mistress and she was just someone whom he undoubtedly still fancied but probably rather pitied, an old flame towards whom he felt a sense of obligation, as well, possibly, of desire?

Yet, about one thing Pierre was right. She could not possibly live in an apartment like the one they'd just seen near the Gare du Nord. No one would visit her there. She would be an outcast from the social scene. She would have no friends. She would hate it. But property even to rent in Paris was very expensive and she would never be able to afford the sort of place where she'd be happy.

Night was falling. It had started to rain. Desolate, uncertain and rather frightened Tina at last reached the luxury of her hotel and hurried inside.

*   *   *

Buddy raked all the leaves into a pile and then tossed them into a wheelbarrow which he trundled to the bottom of the garden. There he added the leaves to a stack out of which he intended to make a bonfire. It was too wet to light one. That would have to wait until the weather improved. He got a stiff broom and began to sweep the path leading to

162

the back door of the cottage, and then he put it aside and went in.

Louise had not been gone very long but even now it had a desolate, unlived in air.

She was a tidy person, but it was too tidy. Gone were all the bits and pieces associated with her: books, magazines, flowers. She always had fresh flowers on the table in the middle of the room, or a colourful bowl of leaves and twigs, if it was the depths of winter, though she could always seem to find something in flower at the garden centre.

In the kitchen everything was static; the floor tiles clean as though no one had trodden on them for years.

Buddy wandered upstairs and paused before going into her bedroom, as though it was somehow a sacred, forbidden place. In fact, the only time he'd been there was when he rushed in after hearing she had been taken ill and found Steve and Tina there too.

He had never slept with her. He wished he had. Now he felt he never would. The parameters, such as they were, had been changed and she had never recognised him for what he was: a sincere, ardent suitor. Someone who loved her, but whose love she could not return.

Feeling like an intruder he gently pushed open the door and looked inside. The bed was covered by a quilt, the dressing table had a few objects on it, but otherwise was bereft of any personal possessions, no pots of cream or lipsticks. But Louise was not one for make-up. In fact he didn't think she wore it at all.

There was, in fact, nothing artificial about Louise. She was just foolish, with a streak perhaps

163

of madness he couldn't comprehend.

Buddy went over to the window and looked out onto the front of the cottage. In the distance he could see the gates of Poynton Manor. It was a small close-knit community and it would have seemed so right for him and Louise to have married, had children and settled in a place where they were known, and maybe loved. Why couldn't she have seen that? What disease had made her so recklessly enamoured of Steve?

Buddy had been born only five miles away at the farm where he now lived: a local man, indeed his family known for generations.

Louise would have been, *was*, so suitable for this environment, this kind of lifestyle. She was a country girl with country ways, unaffected, rather abrupt, but of such sterling quality that it was unbelievable she had fallen for Steve Lockwood the way she had and was about to bear his child. To all intents and purposes they were now living together at the manor.

That had caused a scandal even more than the abrupt departure of his wife, and people thought less of Steve Lockwood and far, far less of Louise because she was a woman. In small rural communities such things were noticed and most people, certainly the older generation, thought that they mattered.

Even if Louise ever came back and tried to live normally in her cottage the way she had before nothing would ever be the same.

Buddy gave a heavy sigh, went downstairs, had a final look round and went out the way he had come through the back door, locking it behind him. He had promised Louise to keep an eye on the place

164

and to look in and see if there was any post. There was nothing. He knew quite well that even without being asked the postman would now deliver it to the manor.

Buddy put away the broom, the rake and fork in the woodshed, upended the wheelbarrow and tilted it on its side, and went round to the front to let himself out by the garden gate. He was closing it when a woman carrying a basket, who had just passed the cottage, turned her head.

'Oh, Buddy!' she cried, 'I didn't expect to see you.'

'How are you Dorothy?' Buddy said politely, fastening the catch on the gate.

'Louise isn't there is she?' Dorothy said, looking surprised.

Buddy shook his head.

'I'm just keeping an eye on things for her.'

They walked along in silence for a moment then Dorothy said, 'Will she be coming back do you think?'

Buddy shrugged.

'I suppose you don't know, do you Buddy? No more than anyone else.'

'That's right.'

'It's a very *odd* situation isn't it?'

Buddy nodded again.

'A man of few words I see,' Dorothy said with a smile.

Buddy stopped and looked at her.

'Well, I don't know and that's the truth. I don't think she knows herself.'

Dorothy looked at him wide-eyed. She was rather a pretty woman, maybe a year or two his senior, as was Louise. She had well spaced blue eyes and rather pretty curly black hair. The eyes were surprising because they made her look Irish and he knew she wasn't, though her husband was, or rather her ex-husband as he'd heard she was divorced. Like Louise she had a fresh, open face and wore just a touch of lipstick, perhaps some foundation or powder, he didn't really know about these things. In fact all in all he was generally very ignorant about women, and Louise with her lack of pretension had made him feel comfortable. Now his attention turned to Dorothy.

Dorothy smiled sympathetically and put a hand on his arm. 'I suppose you're upset, Buddy? I know I shouldn't ask . . .'

'Oh, that's alright. I thought this thing with Steve would pass and it didn't. It got worse.'

'And now she is to have his baby.' Dorothy lowered her voice though there was no one about. The local children were still in school and the village seemed deserted except for them.

Buddy nodded.

'Will she bring it back to the cottage or . . .' Dorothy's eyes sidled towards the main gates of the manor, 'or will she stay there?'

Buddy looked puzzled. 'Well, whatever happens I don't think she'd bring it back to the cottage. I mean . . .' He looked at her. 'You *do* know the baby is not Louise's, don't you?'

Now it was Dorothy's turn to express shock. 'How do you mean?'

Buddy struggled for words. 'I don't know exactly how to put this but the baby is Tina and Steve's. Louise offered to act as a surrogate mother because Tina couldn't carry a baby.'

Dorothy uttered a long low whistle.

'Well, I don't know. She never said a *word*. I suppose she wanted me to believe . . .'

Buddy looked abashed. 'Maybe I shouldn't have spoken.' Yet he was glad he had. Louise, with all her little secrets even from her friends. She'd wanted people to think the baby was hers, as well as Steve's, and something in him took a savage delight in destroying this myth.

'It explains a lot,' Dorothy was saying, almost to herself. 'There were some things I didn't quite understand.'

'You had better not let her know I told you.'

'Oh, I shan't. I wouldn't *dream* of it. Anyway she hardly ever comes into the shop. She's due any moment now you know.'

They had reached the gates of the manor without Buddy being aware of where they were going. There was something warm and comforting about being with Dorothy that made him feel she understood him. There certainly was a touch of Louise about her; something solid and down to earth. He was at ease and relaxed with her.

'Would you like to come to the barn dance at the village hall on Saturday?' he asked suddenly. 'It's Jim Rivers and the Merry Monarch Musicians. They say they're very good.'

Dorothy's blue eyes shone with pleasure. 'What a lovely idea,' she said. 'There's nothing I'd like better.'

CHAPTER ELEVEN

Louise walked slowly along the corridor, the cup and saucer balanced in her hand. The soft glow of the wall lights illuminated the highly polished floor. She had to be careful not to slip. When she reached the door of Steve's study she tapped quietly on it, then she turned the handle.

The room was in semi-darkness save for the lamp behind Steve's head, the garish light of the computer screen which had some sort of chart on it which Steve was sitting back studying. He turned round and Louise said rather diffidently, 'I thought you might like a coffee.'

'How kind you are, Louise.' Steve got up and took the cup and saucer from her. 'Have you had any?'

Louise grimaced. 'It gives me heartburn.'

'Here, sit down.' Steve drew up a chair for her and she sat down gratefully.

'I feel hideous,' she said, hands on the large bulge in front of her.

Steve nodded sympathetically. 'It's a difficult time . . . I know Frances . . .' he stopped as though it might be tactless to mention Frances's name. 'Soon be over,' he finished cheerfully.

'Steve . . . what are we going to do?' Louise looked at him earnestly but he was avoiding her eyes. He knew perfectly well what she meant. 'I mean, are you able to get in touch with Tina?'

'Not yet. But I've given instructions to the bank to stop her allowance. She won't be able to draw any money and I don't believe she has much of her own. She spends rather lavishly, as you know. But don't worry. You will be taken care of.'

Louise immediately bridled. 'How do you mean "taken care of"?'

'Looked after. I mentioned a holiday . . .'

'But what if Tina *isn't* here to look after the baby? That changes everything.'

'I know.' Steve ran his hand across his face which suddenly seemed drained of colour. 'I'll get a nanny. I've just been too busy to think of anything. I have had so much on my mind . . .' He turned towards the computer, indicating the screen. 'I have a mass of work and I haven't been making my usual trips abroad. I'm due to go to Australia . . .'

'Australia!' Louise exclaimed.

'I've got business interests there. I'm thinking of buying a vineyard. I don't want to buy it without looking at it.'

Louise wondered angrily for a moment how Steve could put to the back of his mind the fact that she was about to have his baby and his wife had left him. How *could* he be thinking of buying a vineyard *and* going to Australia at a time like this!

Seeing the expression on her face he said, 'Don't look so put out. Everything will be OK. I think after a time of reflection Tina will come back. I assure you we will never cease to be grateful . . .'

Louise could stand it no more. She put her face in her hands and burst into tears.

Immediately Steve was by her side, his arms around her.

'Louise, what *is* it? Please don't be upset.'

'How can I help being upset?' she sobbed. 'You're so cold, so indifferent. I feel I'm ugly and horrible and no one loves me. I feel what I've done

169

is not appreciated, taken for granted. I . . . Oh I wish I'd never done it. I really do. It was a crazy idea, utterly crazy.'

Her distress affected Steve and he sat by her side, tightly holding her hand in an attempt to infuse her with a sense of reassurance he was far from feeling himself. This whole project had taken on the semblance of a nightmare from which one would not wake up.

Very soon there would be a small, live creature for whom he would be responsible until the end of his life.

'Come on,' he said. 'I'll take you up to bed. It's getting late and I have to leave early in the morning.'

'Leave?' Louise said shrilly, once again overcome by panic, eyes that were nearly dry threatening to overflow again.

'I have to go to London for a few days,' Steve said calmly.

'You're surely not going to try and find Tina?'

'Well no . . .' Looking at her it suddenly dawned on Steve that Louise didn't want him to find Tina, didn't *want* Tina to come home again. That was the idea that was really frightening her.

The sense, now, that she seemed to feel she had him to herself seemed rather scary.

However, docilely like a small, obedient child, Louise allowed Steve to lead her from the room, still with his arm round her, and take her upstairs to her bedroom, very slowly one step at a time and then pause for breath. Her heavy, sagging body and slow steps made him realise how imminent the birth was. If Louise was a romancer so was he. Maybe he had hoped it would never happen.

He opened the door to her room and pushed her inside.

'Now, you go and undress and get into bed and I'll come and tuck you up and say goodnight.'

He smiled at her and she smiled back gratefully, her eyes still wet, cheeks stained with tears. More than ever she looked like a small frightened child herself, totally unprepared for motherhood.

Steve went along the corridor to his room and began to get out the things he wanted to take with him: a couple of shirts, washing and shaving kit, socks and pants. He had spare suits at the flat in London so he would travel very light.

He was looking forward so much to having a few days in London, looking up friends, eating out, maybe a show or two.

But in reality he was looking forward, more than he realised, to being away from Poynton and the restrictive, almost overwhelming, even threatening presence of Louise.

He gave her half an hour to compose herself and then went back to her room, tapping on the door before letting himself in. She was lying in bed stiff as a board, looking frightened to death. The large bump in the middle was the child waiting to be born.

Steve sat down again by her side and took her hand.

'Do you feel better now?' he asked gently.

'Better,' she nodded several times. 'Better but frightened.'

'Why are you frightened?'

'Without you. I will be frightened here on my own. I didn't know you were going away.'

'Only a few days. I have so much to do. Look,

171

shall I ask Buddy if he would come and stay while I'm gone?'

'Oh no. I don't want Buddy,' she said quickly.

His heart sank. 'But I thought you *liked* Buddy?'

'Buddy doesn't understand. Doesn't approve.' She glanced at him slyly. 'Frankly he doesn't like you very much.'

Steve surprised himself by the extent of his own indignation.

'Why doesn't Buddy like me?' he demanded.

'He's jealous of you.'

'But there's no need.'

Louise suddenly grabbed his hand and looked into his eyes. 'You do *love* me don't you Steve? Say it.'

'Well . . .' Steve faltered, 'I like you very much. I'm very *fond* of you, Louise.'

'But that's not the same as love,' Louise said, petulantly disengaging her hand. 'I thought that was why you wanted me to stay here with you.'

'But *you* suggested you stay here,' he said indignantly.

'You didn't oppose it.'

'Of course I didn't. You said you felt unsafe on your own. You know really, Louise . . .' He leaned forward ready to give rein to his frustration and anger, but the expression in her eyes deterred him.

He didn't dare. The time was not yet. Instead he bent over, took her hand again and kissed her on the forehead which he stroked for a few moments until her eyelids fluttered and she appeared ready to sleep. But suddenly her eyes were wide open again, fixed on him, as if in the grip of a new torment.

'Steve, you will be with me at the birth won't

172

you?'

'Of course,' Steve said. 'Not very far away.'

'No, I mean *with* me, holding my hand like now.'

Steve swallowed hard. 'Of course. If that's what you want.'

'Thank you, Steve.' Her clasp tightened and then relaxed as much needed sleep prepared to claim her. 'I love you,' she murmured, 'and one day you will realise how much you love me, and you will be able to say it when you feel really free of Tina.'

*   *   *

Really free of Tina! The woman was living in a dream world. Steve still felt shaken and angered by the events of the previous evening when he left home just after dawn for his drive to London. It had not been necessary to leave so early but he felt that at all costs he wanted to avoid another encounter with the deeply emotional Louise. In fact, he felt at the moment she was dangerously unstable. So unlike that sturdy, practical woman he had come to know and trust and regard as a close friend of the family. Her pregnancy had changed her completely.

Knowing they were both early risers he stopped at the Bartons' cottage to find them having breakfast. They looked up with surprise as he came in and Mrs Barton immediately asked if there was anything wrong.

Steve shook his head reassuringly.

'Oh no. But I have to go to London for a few days and I wondered, Mrs Barton, if you would do me an enormous favour?'

'If I can, Mr L,' Mrs Barton said, getting up from

173

the table and taking her husband's empty plate.

'Would you like something to eat?' Frank Barton asked.

'No thank you,' Steve shook his head. 'It's too early for me, but a cup of tea would be most welcome.'

Mrs Barton looked across at her husband. 'Frank, a cup of tea for Mr L, if you don't mind.'

Frank Barton rose and did as he was told pouring from a large brown pot covered with a cosy on the kitchen bench.

'Thanks very much, Frank.' Steve sat down and took a sip from his cup. 'Mm, very good. I needed that. Mrs Barton, I wondered if you would mind sleeping up at the house while I'm away? Louise is a bit nervous.'

'Why is she nervous?'

'She just is.'

Mrs Barton looked thoughtful. 'That's not like Louise. One time I'd have said she hadn't a nerve in her body.'

'So would I. She's changed. Hopefully she will change back. I expect hormones have a lot to do with it.'

'Hormones!' Mrs Barton snorted as if she found their existence as unbelievable as fairies. They certainly hadn't existed when she'd had her children.

'Seriously,' Steve said earnestly, 'all these changes are considered hormonal but, this apart, the pregnancy has taken its toll on her . . . as it has on us all.' He looked deprecatingly at the housekeeper who pursed her lips and seemed on the verge of saying something. Steve held up his hand.

'I know what you're going to say, Mrs Barton. Please don't say it.'

'Very well, Mr L. I won't.' She sat down at the table, crossed her arms and studied her nails.

'The main thing is that we get Louise over this, and then,' Steve gave an expressive shrug, 'well, you know what a difficult situation it is.'

'Any news of Mrs L?' Mrs Barton enquired pointedly.

Steve shook his head. 'But I hope once the baby is born she'll come round to it. I'm sure she will.' Steve swallowed his tea, looked at his watch, and rose.

'Do you think you'd do that big favour for me?'

'I can't refuse you can I, Mr L?' Mrs Barton said without emotion, but her expression indicated only too clearly that she would if she could, if only he wasn't her employer.

*   *   *

Later that morning Mrs Barton looked up as Louise entered the kitchen. It was well after nine and there were deep furrows under her eyes. 'You look terrible,' she said. 'Are you sure you're alright?'

'Didn't sleep too well.' Louise slumped at the table and put her head in her hands. 'I've got a terrible headache.'

'Do you want any breakfast?'

Louise shook her head. 'A cup of tea would be very nice.'

'Mr Lockwood came to see me this morning,' Mrs Barton said matter-of-factly.

'Oh?'

'He wants me to stay here with you until he returns.'

Louise seemed to cheer up immediately. 'Oh, he's so sweet. He's so caring.' Her eyes shining she seemed to lapse into a reverie, as if oblivious of her surroundings.

Mrs Barton studied her intently for a few moments then she put a cup and saucer in front of her. 'Louise, you seem to me like a girl who doesn't have any sense.'

'I don't know what you mean?' Louise said grumpily.

'You seem to think Mr Lockwood cares more for you than he does.'

'Of *course* he cares for me.' Her tone was indignant. 'Look how concerned he is to make sure I'm alright while he's away. Last night he told me he loved me. What more could you want?'

'He told you that?' Mrs Barton's tone was deeply sceptical.

'Yes.'

'You wrung it out of him I suppose.'

'I did *not* wring it out of him,' Louise replied heatedly. 'What a horrible thing to say.' She sat back with a smug expression on her face. 'You'll see. Once that baby is born things will settle and he will know where his responsibilities are and why.'

'I'll say no more.' Mrs Barton turned to the sink. 'I just hope you're not in for a nasty surprise.'

*   *   *

The trouble, Louise thought, with people like Mrs Barton was that they were so old-fashioned. They believed in fidelity and marriage and to them

176

having a child for someone else was repulsive. But times had moved on. She realised Steve was at some sort of crossroads and she accepted this because she felt she had helped to propel him into making a decision he should have made a long time ago. He should get a divorce from Tina. Maybe that was why he had gone to London.

She wandered along the corridor towards his study and peeped inside. Everything was as it had been the night before with the picture saver on the monitor showing stars and planets shooting across the sky. She watched it in fascination for several moments as it seemed a reflection of her own life. Everything revolving and changing. Elation and confidence one moment, despair and depression the next.

She felt a renewed surge of confidence as she had last night when Steve kissed her and held her hand as she pretended to sleep.

After he had turned out the light and crept out of the room she had lain there conscious of a deep sense of fulfilment, knowing that Steve surely loved her as much as she loved him. Well, perhaps not quite as much, yet, but he would. Once she had had the baby he would find her attractive again and the home she would make for their child would be one of harmony and peace.

And yet . . . slumped in Steve's chair in front of the monitor she experienced a moment of doubt; technically the baby wasn't hers even if emotionally and physically she felt it was. The main thing was that, in Tina's absence, she would bond with it and give it all the love a natural mother could give a child.

After all it was to her that it owed its life.

Without her it could not exist. And she put a hand on her stomach and softly crooned a little song to herself.

* * *

Pierre de Marly leaned across the table of the crowded fashionable Left Bank restaurant and reached for Tina's hand.

'What did you think? Tell me you liked it.'

'Oh, it was lovely . . .' Her voice faltered. No doubt that it was a superb apartment in the Rue de Sèvres not far from Les Invalides. It had once been a grand *hôtel particulier* now turned into expensive apartments with a lift, a uniformed concièrge and courtyard. The previous tenant had been an American diplomat and the furniture was authentic antique. Tina had not even dared to ask the rent.

'But . . . ?' Pierre's aristocratic features expressed concern.

'But I have not made up my mind.'

'I can't wait for ever Tina.' Pierre let go of her hand, a trace of irritation creasing his normally imperturbable brow.

'No. I know. I just hate the thought of being a kept woman.'

'Is that all?' Now the expression changed to one of relief. 'That is easily settled. I will make you an allowance with which . . .'

'That is *still* being a kept woman.'

Pierre lowered his voice. 'But *are* you not a kept woman already? Even a married woman without her own fortune is, in a sense, kept. Does not Steve keep you body and soul, so much so that he cut off your allowance making you penniless?' A note of

178

sarcasm had entered his voice. 'It seems to me, my dear, that you have not much choice . . .'

A movement caused Pierre to look up and his expression changed once again to one of welcome as a tall, dark haired woman stood just behind Tina looking at her with astonishment. 'Is it . . .' she began and as Tina turned she cried out, 'I knew it was. Tina my dear, dear friend,' and she stooped to embrace her while Tina, recovering from her own surprise, returned the embrace.

'Edwige . . .' They both kissed and the man standing with Edwige bowed and shook hands.

'Antoine Pelerin-Bouchard, *Marquis* Pelerin-Bouchard.'

'How do you do?' Tina held out a hand which the tall, distinguished looking man bent and kissed.

'*Enchanté*, Madame.'

'Pierre de Marly.' Edwige continued her introductions and the two men shook hands.

'Are you arriving or leaving?' Tina enquired.

'We're just leaving. How long are you in Paris?'

'I don't know.' Tina looked momentarily confused. 'I haven't decided.'

Edwige opened a small black evening bag and produced a card.

'Telephone me,' she commanded, 'and don't you dare leave Paris without doing it.'

'I promise.' Tina tucked the card into the pocket of her own bag and as her old friend turned she blew her a kiss.

'Fancy, Edwige . . .' she said shaking her head. 'She is just as beautiful.'

'And still as successful.' Pierre leaned across the table to pour more wine into her glass. 'But now she models only for the older woman, you understand?'

'She must be forty,' Tina murmured.

'Oh, at least. She has been very fortunate in keeping both her looks and her job. How long is it since you worked, my dear?'

'Ten years,' Tina ticked them off on her fingers. 'I never worked after I was married. I don't think I could resume it again.'

'But you are still beautiful.'

'But without the contacts. Maybe if I took up Edwige's invitation to telephone . . .' she peered in her handbag to look again at her card.

'But there is no need,' Pierre said, in a wheedling tone, leaning earnestly across the table. 'You know that. Now, when will you give me your answer?'

'Soon.' Tina leaned back looking at him with a dazzling, slightly tantalising smile. 'I promise.'

*   *   *

Tina took in the view from the window of Edwige Constantine's apartment; the river as it divided in two to wend its way either side of Île de la Cité, the dome of the Pantheon, the roofs of the old houses and buildings of the Left Bank, above all the glorious twin towers of the Cathedral of Notre Dame almost opposite. It was a fabulous position.

'It's gorgeous,' she breathed at last turning to her friend. 'How long have you lived here?'

'Since my last divorce. It was part of the settlement.'

Edwige nonchalantly put a glass of wine in Tina's hand and then lightly stroked her shoulder with the tip of a beautifully manicured, scarlet nail.

'It is wonderful to see you again. We should

never have lost touch.'

'So much has happened,' Tina said, taking a sip of the cool wine.

It was nearly dusk and the two women had been talking for hours, starting with lunch at a small restaurant round the corner from Edwige's apartment on the Ile Saint-Louis. In that time they had exchanged life stories—and what lives they had been! Both married twice, Edwige's marriages ending in acrimonious divorces. She was now single, childless and with a wealthy lover who, like Pierre, was also married. The only older unmarried men in Paris were gay. By any standards she had retained her beauty. She looked haughty, mysterious, unattainable and her almost Sphinx-like features—high cheekbones, velvety brown eyes, red lips, black hair drawn tightly back from her forehead into a large chignon at the back— ensured her a steady stream of admirers of all ages and both sexes.

However, unlike Tina, Edwige was a woman of independent means who had amassed a large fortune not only from her two divorces but from her career in her heyday as the favourite model of two or three of the most famous couture houses. Now in her forties she modelled styles for the still fashionable, and perhaps even more wealthy, older woman. As well as her Paris apartment she had another in Palm Beach and a farmhouse in Provence.

She was dark, slim, incredibly elegant, tall even for a model. Her face, however, had that lived-in allure of the woman of experience that enables its owner to resist the temptation of the plastic surgeon's knife. She had enough self-confidence

181

not to want to look like forty apeing twenty. She wanted to look like a forty-year-old, proud of being her age and having lived the life she had, but still able to take care of herself. That encouraged older women and boosted their self-esteem as much as anything.

The two had been great friends when Tina had her first modelling job seventeen years before, even though there were five years or so difference in their ages. But they had lost touch, and very much water had since flowed under the bridges of Paris.

'Tell me about Pierre.' Edwige removed her hand from Tina's shoulder and, glass in hand, sat on a chair near the window overlooking the wonderful view. 'It's ages since I saw him. He is just as attractive, I must say.' She looked archly at her friend.

'Nothing to tell.' Slowly Tina turned from the view to face her, 'except that he wants me to resume our affair.'

'Oh? Is that all? I'm surprised you have not already.'

'I do love Steve.'

'But this business with the child is *terrible*.' Edwige, appearing genuinely shocked, struck her forehead with her hand. '*Quel désastre.*'

'Yes it is disastrous. But it's easy to be wise after the event, oh so easy.'

Edwige nodded. 'Of course. I understand, but what are you going to do now?'

'Well, I heard from the bank that Steve has blocked my allowance. If I want to resume it—and they were very polite and tactful—I have to get in touch with *him*. They were sure it was just a "temporary misunderstanding". Unlike you I have

182

no money of my own. I am very near the end of what little I have. Pierre would like to . . .' she paused momentarily, 'offer me help. We saw a lovely apartment the other day in the Rue de Sèvres. I dared not ask the rent. You know what I mean?'

'I know,' Edwige said softly. 'You do not want to sell yourself to him?'

'No, I do not.'

'In that case,' Edwige patted the seat beside her, inviting Tina to sit down, 'you must come and stay with me until you make up your mind.'

'Oh, but . . .'

'No buts. I insist.' She waved a hand airily round the room. 'There is plenty of space and that way you can make up your own mind and not compromise your relationship with your husband.' She regarded Tina gravely. 'By the way, he sounds very nice.'

'He is,' Tina said quietly, fearing herself on the verge of tears, 'that's the trouble. If I started an affair with Pierre, Steve would never have me back. That would be utterly and finally the end.'

*   *   *

Everyone seemed to be gearing up for Christmas. The television advertisements were all about gifts to buy, places to visit, things to see during the festive season, and trade was quite brisk in the shop. Louise had her own special chair behind the counter and stayed there most of the day while Dorothy wrapped gifts, sorted out enquiries, made suggestions for presents and saw to the stock. The tea room remained open and from twelve noon onwards there was a brisk trade.

But by five Louise was tired, longing for closing time. Susan had put a CLOSED notice on the door of the restaurant and the last stragglers were finishing their tea, emerging staggering under the weight of their purchases tucked into large carriers printed with the Poynton crest.

'Merry Christmas' they cried happily from the door where Dorothy stood ready to lock up after the last one had left.

'Thank goodness today's over,' Louise said beginning to cash up as Dorothy was finally able to lock the door.

'Weary, are you?' Dorothy enquired sympathetically.

Louise nodded. 'Tired. Oh, I *wish* Steve would hurry up and come back or this baby will be born without him.'

'Where *is* Steve exactly?' Dorothy asked curiously.

'In London. He says he has a lot of business.' Louise sighed deeply. 'I suppose one must believe him.'

'Don't you?'

'I suppose he has if he says he has,' Louise's tone was grudging. 'But you would have thought he would clear the decks just when his baby is due.'

Both women looked towards the door as loud knocks sounded from the other side.

'Someone's forgotten something I expect,' Dorothy said with a laugh and went to unlock the door. She stepped aside feigning surprise as Buddy appeared, face red from the cold, a woolly hat pulled well down over his ears.

'Buddy!' Louise greeted him with a smile of

welcome. 'How nice to see you. Everything alright at the cottage?'

'Everything's fine, Louise. I brought up some post and left it with Duncan. I asked him to pop it into the house on his way home.'

'Why, didn't you expect to see me?' Now it was Louise's turn to look surprised.

'Well . . . not exactly. I thought you'd be putting your feet up. Actually I came to collect Dorothy. We're going into Yeovil for late-night shopping.'

'Oh, I see.' Louise noted the proprietorial 'we'. She acknowledged to herself a sense of chagrin as well as shock. 'Well, I won't keep you.' She smiled at Dorothy. 'I'll finish cashing up.'

'Are you sure?' Dorothy looked abashed.

'Quite sure,' Louise said. 'You run along and enjoy yourselves.'

'We might take in a meal,' Buddy said.

'Sounds like a good idea.' Louise realised now something she seemed to have missed before; there was a real change in Buddy. He no longer looked at her in that special way. He was giving her a dose of her own medicine.

Well, it didn't matter. Just as well that he had someone else. He would never ever have taken the place of Steve, though it had been useful to have him around, and it really was quite nice to be admired, to be the subject of a dog-like devotion which, at the time, one had failed to appreciate.

She had taken Buddy and his goodness for granted. Now she realised she could no more.

Rather sadly she crossed the shop floor after they had gone and locked the main door. Then she put out the lights and went through the side door into the garden from which there was a path

185

leading to the house.

Now it was quite dark, all the lights in the centre were out. Duncan had obviously gone home and Susan had left the restaurant. There was no light to guide her, but Louise was by now perfectly familiar with the way and the lights of the house were like a welcoming beacon, except that there would be no one there to greet her.

She knew how desolate and empty it was without Steve. Mrs Barton would have gone too, leaving her meal in the oven, and there would be nothing for her to do all evening except watch the television, shifting uncomfortably in her chair, and then making her way to bed.

Mrs Barton had never hidden her contempt for Louise and her disapproval of the situation she was in, and made no attempt to be a companion to her. Just before ten Mrs Barton would return and go to the room made up for her on the second floor.

She might or she might not say 'goodnight', but she clearly found the duty onerous and Louise was sorry that Steve had ever asked her.

It was a cold but dry evening, the stars very bright in the night sky. Christmas was coming, a time of joy for many but not for Louise Hamilton. She felt no sense of the spirit of Christmas, no thrill of anticipation, just a mild feeling of dread that grew more acute with every day that passed. All she wanted now was for it to be over.

She pushed open the kitchen door. A light had been left on and, sure enough, her dinner was on the hot plate. It was a casserole of something or other with vegetables and a suet pudding with custard for afters. A knife, fork and spoon were set on the table together with a side plate, salt and pepper and a glass for water. It would be nice to have company for her meal, but Mrs Barton always made a point of the necessity of getting home to cook for Frank.

Better than ever it would be nice to have Steve; his absence was that much harder to take.

Louise went up to her room and lay for some time on the bed. She was vaguely nauseous and off her food. She didn't feel like doing anything. She felt extremely bloated and uncomfortable, and also rather hot as if she were feverish. She supposed she dozed for a few moments, maybe longer, and then she was awoken by a sharp pain which made her sit upright on the bed and clutch her stomach with both hands. This was followed by another sharp pain and then another, and then there was a rush of liquid from between her legs and she knew that the waters had broken and the birth was imminent. She could delay no longer.

With trembling hands she lifted the phone and dialled Mrs Barton's number. It rang and rang until finally she put the receiver down. She knew Buddy was out with Dorothy. She didn't know Duncan's new telephone number and she had no idea where Steve was. There was no one else she felt able to call in a crisis.

Louise felt utterly, crushingly frightened, completely alone as she dialled the ambulance service and said it was an emergency.

CHAPTER TWELVE

Steve still found his ex-wife, Frances, attractive. He thought that if she hadn't gone off with another man they would even now still be married, living together with their two children and everything would be hunky-dory. He would thus never have found himself in the pickle that he was.

She was not as beautiful as Tina, with rather robust, well-bred Sloaney-type good looks. She was of medium height with thick, springy black hair, rather untidily kept, blue eyes, a curved good-humoured mouth and a determined dimple in the chin. She was the sort of woman who looked as though she had been bred for outdoor pursuits, and one of the attractions of being married to Steve had been that she could ride and hunt to her heart's content, activities that held no attraction at all for Tina, who preferred the warm salons of couture houses. In fact the man she eloped with was a master of hounds, and in the season they spent as much time as they could in the country killing wild, defenceless animals.

Frances had interrupted her sporting activities to come up to London to do some Christmas shopping. She also had a house in Kent, which was where the children were, so that when Steve asked to come round and see her he found her alone. He hadn't wasted a moment in spilling out his troubles to Frances who, in common with many people told of the situation, found it inexplicable.

Steve and Frances had shared bread and cheese and half a bottle of wine, and talked about the children and the situation with Louise—which Frances had known about—and Tina, which she hadn't. Frances had always remained fond of Steve. To her mind the marriage had foundered not for any fundamental incompatability but, in addition to his lack of enthusiasm for blood sports, on his inability to take time off from work either to give more time to his family or enjoy himself. Her present husband, who was a non-executive director of a number of companies which paid him a fortune for doing very little, was in the happy position of mainly being able to give himself up to relaxing pastimes.

It was nearly three in the afternoon and Steve talked about leaving.

'I was sorry not to see the kids,' he said, getting up from the table. 'Will I before Christmas?'

Frances frowned. 'Not unless you come down to Ashbury. We'd love to see you.' She put a hand on his arm. 'Really, Steve. Come and relax for a few days. You're welcome to spend Christmas with us if you like . . .'

'Well . . . hardly . . . unfortunately. I think it would look bad. The baby is due at any minute.'

Frances was about to say something when the telephone rang, cutting her short, and she went into the hall to answer it. Steve could hear her talking and then in a few seconds she was back.

'That was Mrs Barton,' she said. 'Apparently that girl has gone into labour. She asked if I knew where you were.'

'Oh *God*!' Steve sat down by the table and put his head in his hands. 'What did you say?' he asked finally, looking up.

'I said I didn't know where you were.'

'That was decent of you.'

'But Steve, you must see her.' Looking serious, rather formidable, Frances sat opposite him. 'You can't *ignore* it. They've tried the Albany, your mobile, and all they get is the answerphone. Hadn't you better go?'

'Really, I can't face it.'

'But Steve, it was *you* who started it.'

'*She* started it,' Steve objected. 'It was Louise's suggestion to which we foolishly assented.' He wearily ran his hands over his face. 'I am really ashamed of myself, but I can't face it. Not just now. She wants me to hold her hand in labour. I can't imagine anything more awful.'

Frances tightly pressed his arm. 'Poor old Steve. You did get yourself in a mess didn't you? The girl is clearly in love with you.'

'That's what everyone said. At the time I couldn't see it myself. I've realised it since, and she has become an irritant to me. On the other hand I also feel guilty and sorry for her.' He looked down at the floor. 'It seems an impossible situation and I really don't know what to do. A baby I don't now want with a woman I no longer even really like, and an absent wife who won't even tell me where she is. Work that out if you can.'

He glanced up at Frances who was studying her watch, her mind clearly now on other things. 'I must go. I have a hair appointment at three-thirty. If I were you I'd get back to Mrs Barton. You can't ignore what's happening for ever. It's not fair, Steve. It's not worthy of you. For one thing it's not fair on the child and, whether you like it or not, it *is* yours.'

There was a curious, almost eerie stillness in the room, broken by a scarcely audible gurgle which brought Louise sharply back to reality. She looked down at the baby in the crib beside her bed and then looked hurriedly away again.

'Stranger,' she thought, 'little stranger'. She had so thought she would bond with her and love her immediately, but the opposite had been the case. She thought it was because Steve had been absent, that everything would have been different if he had kept his word and been with her.

It had been a long labour, but in the end an easy birth. However, it had been her alone, except that is for the midwife and once a doctor had popped his head round the door of the delivery room to be sure that all was well. It had been lonely. The hours of labour had been among the most lonely in her life.

She had bitterly reflected on all the care and fuss lavished on her at the beginning when she was the centre of attention; a private room in a special clinic, compared to the isolation she felt now, the despair that no one loved her or cared about her.

She'd been surrounded by other women in various stages of labour with their spouses or partners uttering words of encouragement, helping them with breathing exercises, holding their hands, wiping their brows; but not her. She'd laboured alone except for the occasional visit of the midwife or a nurse. They kept on changing shifts and she hardly ever saw the same one twice. There was a big shortage of nurses, so many of them came from agencies. A perfect stranger ultimately delivered the baby.

She'd wiped her own brow and done her own breathing exercises. No one to hold her hand.

No Steve, no Buddy, no anyone. Never in her life had she felt so alone, and when the cause of all this trouble arrived it was not even hers. She was big, blue-eyed with fluffy blonde hair, even at birth, despite all the wrinkles, the spitting image of Tina.

'Is she like your husband?' one of the nurses had asked doubtfully, comparing Louise with the baby beside her. Louise had nodded. Her husband, she had explained on admission, was abroad on business.

The first visitors had been Buddy and Dorothy who brought flowers, couldn't think what to say and didn't stay long. Then Duncan came with more flowers. He had been monosyllabic too, and finally Frank Barton put his nose in and said his wife was busy looking after the manor and trying to contact Steve. He didn't bring anything and stayed all of five minutes, looking awkward and ill at ease.

That was yesterday and forty-eight hours later there was still no sign of the baby's father.

There were three other mothers on the ward but Louise didn't speak to any of them. Now two of them were asleep and one was absent. The room was so still, except for the gurgling, happy baby beside her.

When they were all awake, from time to time one of the women would wander over, carrying her baby, and peer into the cot.

'Pretty isn't she?' she'd say.

Louise would ignore them.

A nurse had asked her if she felt depressed and she'd shaken her head.

Soon now it would be feeding time and the two mothers woke up. Bottles were being produced, or those mothers feeding their children would sit by their beds with bosoms proudly bared and infants sucking away.

There was an air of good-natured jollity in the ward which Louise hated: all these happy, contented women with husbands or partners, people who loved them popping in and out. Here was she: a freak, not even the natural mother of the child she'd borne.

'Would you like to have a go at feeding baby today, Mrs Hamilton?' Nurse, with a bright, rather false smile on her face, gently lifted the baby from the crib and cradled her.

'No thank you,' Louise said.

'Have you thought about why not?' Nurse, another stranger she hadn't seen before, sat on the side of the bed, baby in her arms. 'It is the natural thing, you know.'

'Because I don't want to.' Louise gazed at her steely-eyed. 'You see, she's not mine.'

'Oh!' Nurse, who was a temporary from an agency, appeared nonplussed. 'Would you like to see the doctor and discuss your problem with him?'

'I don't have any problem,' Louise replied and turned her back to the nurse, her face to the wall. 'I wish I were dead.'

Nurse rose from the bed and took the baby away with her to a room off the ward where, sitting on a chair, she fed her from a bottle. Then, after returning baby to the crib, she went to report her conversation to the ward sister. Clearly they thought Louise was seriously depressed.

Steve, carrying a large bunch of flowers, stood on the threshold of the four-bed ward and immediately saw Louise on her side, apparently fast asleep. He tiptoed across to the bed and quietly placed the flowers on the locker beside it. Then, his heart in his mouth, he bent down and, gently pulling the blanket back, saw a beautiful child with pink cheeks and blue eyes smiling up at him, little fists raised in the air as if in greeting, almost as though she was already intent on relishing and enjoying life.

At that cataclysmic moment all Steve Lockwood's misgivings appeared to evaporate, all his doubts and forebodings vanished and he drew the blanket right back and picking up the baby cradled her, his eyes full of tears.

When he looked up Louise was sitting up in bed staring at him.

'Thank you,' he said. 'She's beautiful isn't she?'

'How do you know it is a girl?'

'She's so like Tina.'

Louise's mouth set in a grim line. 'What kept you, Steve? You've been away nearly a week.'

'I had a lot of business abroad,' he lied. 'I only received the message when I got back.'

'Did you see Tina?' Louise asked suspiciously.

Steve shook his head. 'No. I still don't know where she is.'

'Then what are you going to *do*, Steve?'

'I'm going to take her and love her. I love her already,' and he kissed her cheek relishing the lovely warm baby smell which recalled the birth of his other children, and hugged her once again

194

before putting the baby tenderly back in her crib and covering her carefully.

The ward sister appeared at his side, all smiles.

'Back are we, Mr Hamilton? Isn't she lovely?'

'Gorgeous,' Steve enthused. Then he looked guiltily across at Louise. 'I'm sorry I missed the birth. It was a little bit early.'

'I think the doctor would rather like to have a word with you, Mr Hamilton.' Sister gave Steve a meaningful look and, glancing at the still stony-eyed Louise, he got up and followed Sister to a small room off the ward where a white-coated doctor sat at a desk writing. As soon as Steve entered he put aside what he was doing and came towards him, hand outstretched.

'Mr Hamilton,' he said and then stopped, a look of enquiry on his face. 'Or is it?'

'Lockwood, Steve Lockwood.' Steve shook his hand.

'And I'm Anthony Bishop, obstetric registrar. Do sit down.' He indicated a chair while Sister hovered.

'Would you like me to stay, Doctor?'

'I think you'd better. Do you mind, Mr Hamilton?'

'Lockwood,' Steve corrected him. 'Not at all.'

The doctor resumed his seat. 'We know of course that Louise is a surrogate mother. She seems to be having difficulties coping.'

'I'm sorry. I should have been here.'

'She is depressed, and anxious to distance herself from the baby. I must say we have had no experience of surrogacy here, but I would think it was a not uncommon reaction. Is your wife . . .' he looked enquiringly up at Steve.

195

'My wife, I'm afraid, decided some time ago that it was a situation she couldn't face. There was some animosity between her and Louise.'

'But it is your wife's baby?'

'Oh yes.'

The doctor looked again at his file, turning over the pages of notes. 'I have a note here from the fertility centre. I rather feel this is something they should have dealt with themselves. She should have had the baby there. They would know how to handle it.'

Steve seemed bewildered. 'But Louise seemed so *well*, so . . . looking forward to the birth. In fact, I was worried that she seemed to regard the baby as her own.'

'Well, she doesn't now. She is not trying to bond with her at all, and this makes us anxious, as the first days are so important. Is your wife . . .' the doctor looked up, 'around?'

'Unfortunately not at the moment. But I am perfectly prepared to look after my child and make provision for her.'

'And what about Louise? She is ready to leave the hospital any time you like. What will you do with her, and the baby then? Have you decided Mr Lockwood?'

*   *   *

Louise said 'I'm sorry Steve.'

'Nothing to apologise for. I should have been there.'

'You should have kept in touch.'

'I know.'

'I think you did it deliberately.'

'Not at all. I was genuinely detained. I know this is a very important matter. I don't deny it for a moment, but I have a lot of business interests worldwide that need my attention or they'll go under. This building fiasco at Poynton has demanded a lot more of my time than I ever thought I'd have to give it.'

'And I count for nothing.' Louise gazed at him stormily.

Steve felt apprehensive, miserable, above all, weary. They had only been back from the hospital a few hours and already he felt lost, out of his depth, with Louise's swift changes of mood; hostile one moment, embarrassingly self-deprecatory the next.

'I think I'll go and see if Mrs Barton has arrived,' he said. 'I can't think what's happened to her.'

'You're just making excuses, Steve.'

'Oh, for heaven's sake, Louise! Don't make it all so difficult. It *is* a very difficult time for both of us, but there is no need to make it any worse than it is.' And he hurried out of the drawing room while Louise gazed abjectly after him.

She felt so empty inside. So used, and abused. What should have been a happy time, she and the baby together with Steve, planning their lives, was a disaster. She knew her responses were erratic but she felt unable to help herself; there was so much anger and resentment bubbling away under her desire to please.

After a few minutes Steve returned, a letter in his hand. Louise could tell from his face that something was amiss. He sat down and read the letter again, then passed it to her. 'Mrs Barton doesn't want to work here any more. Doesn't

197

approve.'

The letter was from her husband Frank.

Dear Mr Lockwood,

My wife has asked me to write and tender her resignation as your housekeeper. She does this with regret being fond of you and Mrs L and your two children, but feels, the present circumstances being what they are, that she had no alternative. She will forgo wages in lieu of notice.

Yours sincerely,

Frank Barton.

'It's me,' Louise said. 'She never approved.'

'I can't understand such prejudice,' Steve looked bewildered.

'Can't you?' Louise said bitterly. 'I can. Here you and I are together with a baby that isn't mine, but is yours by an absent wife. You can't expect working class people to understand that.'

Steve ignored the class bias. He thought a lot of people, working class or otherwise, might share Mrs Barton's feelings. 'What are we going to do?'

'Nothing,' Louise said prosaically. 'What can we do?'

'I think I'll ask Dorothy O'Brien if she'll step in. After all the shop will soon be closed until Easter. She might be glad of the money. She has two children. She'll know how to look after babies.'

'And I don't?'

'Well, you'll learn with her help. But I thought you couldn't bond with baby?'

'I can if you help me,' Louise said defensively. 'I don't see why we need Dorothy here.'

'Because . . .' Steve felt his patience wearing

thin. 'Oh Louise, can't you see sense? Because of what people will say. I find myself in an intolerable position.'

'*You* find yourself in an intolerable position?' Louise resumed the stormy mode, tears coursing down her cheeks. 'What the hell about *me*?'

Steve placatingly extended both his hands. 'You must be calm, Louise. We must *both* be calm.'

'You *said* you'd get a nurse for the baby and you've done nothing. You break all your promises, Steve. What am *I* supposed to do? Hang around until I'm dismissed?'

'Oh, don't be so ridiculous.'

As if provoked by his words beyond endurance Louise suddenly flew at him and started to hit him, pummelling his chest until it hurt. He grabbed both her hands and shook her, restraining himself because he felt like throttling her.

'Louise, Louise calm down. This is doing nobody any good, least of all yourself. Think about the baby.'

'Why should *I* think about the baby?'

'Because you gave birth to her. I thought you wanted to be part of the family?'

'A sort of kindly aunt?' Louise said, sneeringly. 'Well that was in the past, Steve. That seems years ago though it was only nine months. Christ!' She threw herself theatrically into a chair, covering her face with both hands. 'I can't really believe now that it ever happened. That *I* could have been so foolish . . . thinking you cared for me, perhaps loved me.'

She stopped her tirade and looked at him.

'That was in your imagination, Louise,' Steve said softly. 'I did care for you . . . but I told you I

199

loved Tina.'

'Then why did she go away?'

'Because,' Steve said as gently as he could, fearing for Louise's state of mind, 'because I think she was a little jealous of you.'

'There!' Louise cried triumphantly, 'she *knew* there was something between us.'

'But there wasn't.' Steve began to sound desperate.

'There was. You know there was, Steve. I could tell by your manner towards me. Don't deny it, please. You were trying to conceal it, but it was obvious . . .'

As she trailed off Steve looked intently at her for a full minute.

'You know, Louise, I think you need treatment,' he said with an air of despair. 'I really do.'

*   *   *

It was after midnight and Steve's emotions had been too ragged to allow him to go to sleep. He lay reading, or trying to make sense of the words jumbled on the page when suddenly he heard the sound of the door handle turning. He froze, put down his book and half got out of bed.

'Who is it?' he called.

After a while a thin reedy voice said,

'Steve, I'm sorry.'

'That's alright.' Steve slumped back on the bed.

'Could you let me in, Steve, to talk about it?'

'Louise,' Steve said tiredly, 'there is *nothing* to talk about. Please go back to bed and go to sleep.'

'I really *am* sorry I was so silly and said those things. I just want to make it alright with you,

200

Steve.'

'But it *is* alright'. He got up and pressed his face against the door thanking heaven he'd taken the precaution of locking it, which he hardly ever did. 'Did you take your sleeping pill?'

'No. I wanted to talk to you.'

'We'll talk in the morning. I'm very tired.' Then, anxiously, 'Is baby with Dorothy?'

'Yes, she's in her room.'

'Good. Now you go back and take that pill and we'll talk again tomorrow.' There was no reply and he thought she'd gone away until there was a fresh tap on the door.

'*Please*, Steve.'

'*No*, Louise.'

'Then I'll sleep on the floor outside your door.'

'That would be very silly. You'll catch cold.' He paused and said after a while, 'Actually, Louise, I don't care if you do. I'm not opening the door, and that's final.'

'I'll kill myself,' she said after another long pause.

He stiffened but, to his surprise, he felt so weary that his sense of fear was diminished. 'I don't think you will,' he said. 'Anyway I'm not opening this door. Go back to bed.'

There was no reply and he pressed his ear against the door listening for the sound of her footsteps, but he heard nothing.

He went back to his bed and fell fast asleep not knowing whether or not Louise was keeping a vigil outside his door, nor caring very much if she was, or if she slit her throat first.

*　　　*　　　*

Dorothy stood for a long time looking at the figure of the woman who had clearly worn herself out weeping and was now fast asleep. Or was she? Had she perhaps heard the door open and was pretending to be asleep, hoping she would go away again? Louise was so duplicitous you never knew the truth.

'Louise,' she said shaking her gently by the shoulder, but Louise didn't stir. 'Louise,' she said again with another gentle shake and Louise said abruptly, 'Go away.'

'It's me, Dorothy.'

'I know. I said "go away".' Louise had not slept until dawn smarting under Steve's rejection a few hours before.

'Louise don't be so *silly*.' Dorothy sat on the side of the bed keeping her hand on Louise's shoulder.

'Silly? I'm not silly. Steve thinks I'm mad.'

'No he doesn't.'

'He said he thought I needed treatment.'

Dorothy was silent. She and Buddy had discussed Louise over and over again and tended to agree with Steve.

'Treatment doesn't mean you're mad.'

'What does it mean then?' Louise, who had lain in a foetal position on the bed, sat upright pushing back her hair, her face still ravaged by tears.

'Just that you need a little bit of help.'

'Help with what?'

'Your feelings for Steve, perhaps.'

'And what about his feelings for me?'

Dorothy remained silent.

'You think he doesn't have them?' Louise demanded.

'He says he doesn't.'

'Oh, you've discussed it, have you?'

'A little. I mean he is anxious about you and thinks it is because of the baby . . . you know hormones. They're all over the place.'

'Wouldn't *you* be in a disturbed state, and wouldn't your hormones be all over the place if you'd had a baby that wasn't yours for someone who didn't appreciate it, and then were discarded as if you were an object?'

'Yes I would, but that is not the case with you. Steve *very* much appreciates what you've done and doesn't mean to discard you. He is fond of you . . .'

'He *told* me he loved me,' Louise insisted in a strong voice.

'He said he didn't mean it, in that way.'

'I think he did and he's suppressing it because he feels guilty about Tina. I know we have a bond. Oh, Dorothy, if Steve would only *admit* he loves me he would be so much happier. I feel then I could begin to love the baby too, and we would all be happy together. *I* am suppressing my own natural feelings because of fear of rejection, of losing her. After all, all the time I was pregnant I felt I loved the baby because it was something I shared with Steve. That's why I was so thrilled when Tina went away. Now he doesn't want to know and that affects the way I feel towards baby.'

Dorothy waited a few minutes until Louise seemed calmer. Her breathing became less heavy and her face less flushed.

'I mean,' Louise went on peevishly, 'how could he stay away from the birth? I relied on him so much. It shows he's not a bit grateful for all I've done, given nine months of my life to having his child. How could he do that to someone he loves?'

Dorothy took a deep breath and said in an even tone, 'I'm sure he is grateful, but he doesn't love you, Louise, not in the way you want, and the sooner you accept that the better.'

'But I *know* he does,' Louise insisted.

'But he can't. Be logical. As you yourself say, what man would behave like that if they loved somebody? He didn't even phone or try to keep in touch, even though he knew the birth was imminent. It's time, Louise, that you made yourself realise what a foolish woman you've been and start making the best of the rest of your life.'

'Go away,' Louise commanded roughly, trying to push her off the bed.

'I'll go, but Steve said to tell you I'll be staying on for the time being to help you look after baby.'

'What about your own children?'

'They've gone to their father. I'll see them on Christmas Day. I'm here to help you and Steve, and together I hope we can sort something out. Otherwise we'll all go round the bend and that won't do anyone any good.'

*   *   *

Dorothy went slowly back downstairs and into the room where Steve waited for her. Baby, who was yet to be given a name, was asleep in her pram watched over by him. He looked up anxiously as Dorothy came in.

'Well,' she said, 'I wasn't able to do much. She's in a bad state. I think you should call the doctor eventually, not today. See how she gets on. I've given her a good straight talking to.'

204

'Oh dear!' Steve looked abashed.

'No, I think she needs it. I really do. She's got herself in a stupid state and must get out of it. Let her sleep it off and perhaps think about what I've told her. I've tried to explain, Steve, that you didn't love her, but she won't believe it. She's got it into her head that you do, and I don't think at the moment anything will dislodge it. It is a difficult period. Let's hope she comes round after Christmas. Things may be better then.'

'But what am I going to do, Dorothy?' Steve sounded so desperate that Dorothy began to fear for his sanity too.

'Why don't you write to Tina?' she suggested. 'Now that the baby is born, is here? Tell her. Plead with her. Ask for a meeting. It's all you can do.'

*　　　*　　　*

Tina strolled back along by the river towards the Ile Saint-Louis, her hand on the letter tucked into her pocket. The Christmas and New Year celebrations were over and Paris was a grey, rather depressing looking city now that the lights had all been taken down and people were struggling back to work. It was also wet and very cold.

Pierre had gone to his family for Christmas, and was not yet back. Edwige had been to countless dinners and parties and was now about to recuperate at her farm in Provence to which she wanted to take Tina.

But Tina didn't want to go. On the other hand she didn't particularly want to stay in Paris. She felt rather lost and alone, missing Steve. Missing him very much. She and Edwige had got on wonderfully well and she had given her a respite from the importunate Pierre; but she couldn't go on living like this and, besides, it would soon be an abuse of a friend's hospitality to stay for over a month without signs of going. She came to the bridge, crossed it, and walked along the narrow street to the other side of the small island. Then she came to the house that contained Edwige's apartment and climbed the stairs. It was a house built in the seventeenth century and considered not structurally robust enough to stand the construction of a lift.

Tina reached the third floor and let herself in. Edwige was sitting in front of the television watching a programme which she immediately switched off as Tina entered.

'I was just about to have some tea,' she said.

'I'll get it,' Tina volunteered. 'Don't forget I know how to make it properly.'

Edwige laughed at a shared joke, sat back in her chair, switched on the television again.

Really she was an ideal companion, Tina thought going into the kitchen and putting on the kettle, relaxed and easy going. She had taught Edwidge to make leaf tea and to warm the pot and stand it to let the tea brew. Edwige drank it with lemon, so she cut a fruit in half then sliced it thinly, putting the slices on a plate. She got milk from the fridge, poured it into a jug, put out cups and saucers and *langues-du-chat* from a tin. As she carried the tray in Edwige zapped off the TV again.

'It's only rubbish,' she said. 'Any news?' She knew Tina had gone for her post.

Tina produced the letter which she had transferred from her coat to the pocket of her trouser suit.

'From Steve,' she said waving it in the air. 'The baby is born.'

'Oh my!' Edwige clapped her hands together, a startled expression on her face. 'What is it?'

'A girl.' Tina unfolded the letter. 'Apparently she looks just like me.'

'Oh, how sweet.' Impulsively Edwige rose from her chair and threw her arms round Tina, embracing her. 'My darling, congratulations, you are a mother!'

'It doesn't feel like it one little bit. It feels strange though.' Tina began to pour and after she had given Edwige her cup and taken her own, sat down. 'It is a very peculiar feeling.'

'For the woman too I imagine,' Edwige said drily.

'Apparently she has not taken it well. Steve is very worried about her.'

'Oh?'

'He thinks she's on the verge of a nervous breakdown. She was always besotted by Steve, only he couldn't see it. I think she imagined she was the real mother of the child. That's what *I* couldn't stand. He's paying for it now. The doctor has given her medication and thinks she ought to see a psychiatrist.' Tina put the letter back in her pocket. 'It's all here in the letter. Reams of it.'

'Depression?'

'And anxiety. She's also aggressive and feels let down. Threatened suicide.'

'Oh my goodness!' Edwige looked concerned. 'What is happening to the poor baby?'

'She's being well taken care of by a friend, a sensible woman with children of her own, and also a friend of Louise.' Tina paused and her face

207

assumed a strange expression. 'The thing is Steve says he loves the baby, and did so from the first moment he saw her.'

Tina smiled shyly and selected a biscuit. 'He says it's because she's so like me.'

'He wants you to go back, of course?'

'Begs me to.'

'And what of the woman—the surrogate?'

Tina shrugged. 'That's the problem. I really don't know what to do.'

Edwige rose and went over to sit by the side of her friend, putting an arm round her.

'Go back to him, my dear. Give it a chance. It is a strange situation, but at last you have a child together. Whether you feel it or not you are a mother. It is your baby not the woman's—I forget her name.'

'Louise.'

'Louise. It is not Louise's baby but clearly she needs some sort of help. Personally I feel sorry for her in a way. It *is* a tragic situation.'

As Tina didn't reply but continued to look thoughtful Edwige continued.

'You know I always regretted not having children. By any means I think I would have done so now. It is too late for me, but you and Steve, by surrogacy, have created a baby. Go back and see her. Love her, as he has. Give them both a chance.'

'What about Louise?' Tina's expression became agonised.

Edwige gave a Gallic shrug. 'You certainly can't share the baby with *her*. It would be disastrous. If I were you I would try and get rid of her, in the nicest possible way of course. It sounds harsh but I think it is best for all concerned. Send her away somewhere. Doesn't everyone have their price, or is that a very cynical thing to say?'

CHAPTER THIRTEEN

Soon the January snows would be gone and the snowdrops would fill the woods with the promise of spring. After that the crocuses would cluster round the bases of the trees, and then it would be daffodil time.

Louise certainly had a spring in her step, a sense of joy in her heart as she made her way along the snowy path from the manor to her cottage on the far side of the village. The future looked good. Her affection for baby—still without a name—was increasing because Steve was so tender and caring towards the child, so sweet to her. There had recently been such a transformation in his attitude since things had settled down.

It was, she thought, as though a crisis in his life had been resolved and at last they could plan their future together.

Louise opened the gate of the cottage, walked up the path and as she reached the door it opened and Buddy stood on the threshold, his face showing as much surprise as hers.

'Why Louise,' he said, 'I was just checking that there were no frozen pipes.'

'That was very nice of you Buddy. I came to do the same thing.' Louise put a hand on his arm and kissed his cheek. 'Happy New Year. I don't think I've seen you since. Why don't you come in and have a cup of coffee?'

'Well,' Buddy hesitated, 'that would be very nice, but I don't think there's any milk.'

'I've got some powdered milk. Always keep it just in case.'

Buddy hadn't seen Louise for a few weeks and was pleased at the apparent change in her. She no longer looked pale and frightened but almost her former, robust self. He had regular reports on her from Dorothy and knew that the situation at the manor had vastly improved since those grim days when she returned home with the baby shortly before Christmas.

It was chilly inside the cottage and Louise hastened to the fireplace where a fire had been laid and put a match to it.

'Won't take long to warm up.' She looked around rubbing her hands. 'Strange how little I see of this place now.'

'Will you . . .' Buddy paused, 'come back do you think?'

'Back?' Louise looked surprised. 'Oh no. Steve and I will be making our lives together with baby . . . strange she still hasn't a name, but Steve can't seem to get round to it.'

'And how is . . .' Buddy paused again, 'baby?'

'She's *lovely*. It took some getting used to. It was bad at first, I expect Dorothy told you. But with Steve so loving and caring, why it's all rubbing off on me.' She looked round again. 'I suppose eventually I'll sell or let this place, but there's plenty of time.' She gazed at Buddy. 'Oh, the coffee! I almost forgot.'

'It's alright I don't want it, really.'

'Oh come on, just for old times' sake.'

Followed by Buddy, Louise went into the kitchen

which was spick and span, put on the kettle and spooned instant coffee into two mugs. 'Odd how things work out isn't it, Buddy?'

'Very odd.' Buddy leaned against the kitchen bench.

'And you've been awfully good,' she continued, 'caring and supportive. I hope things work out for you and Dorothy as they are for me and Steve.'

'I *think* we're going to get married,' Buddy blurted out. 'You know I wanted to marry. The fact is I want to settle down and have a family. The single life no longer seems to suit me.'

'Oh, I'm so glad!' Louise did, indeed, seem genuinely pleased. 'Dorothy is such a treasure. We won't be needing her much longer. Steve and I will have our own children in time, I expect, but we'll always love baby. She's special, I feel I'll love her like my own.' She looked straight into Buddy's eyes. 'Eventually I suppose Steve and I will get married, just like you and Dorothy. I told you it would work out. You never believed me.'

Buddy, embarrassed, said nothing. This was a widely different view of events from the one he was getting from Dorothy. He felt that Louise was fantasising again, but what could he say?

These high spirits of Louise didn't seem altogether natural. Despite her apparent vivacity, her air of certainty, she did still have dark circles under her eyes, evidence of sleepless nights as if she was still haunted by bad dreams. For all her declared happiness somehow Louise did not sound very convincing. He mumbled something about work and quickly finished his coffee. Louise still hadn't finished hers but she didn't seem to mind him going and saw him to the door.

211

They kissed lightly again and she watched him walk down the path to the gate where he turned and gave a brief wave.

She shut the front door and stood looking around her, not quite sure where to begin or even, for the moment, why she'd come.

*   *   *

Dorothy, nodding off beside the baby's crib, jerked her head up as she heard the nursery door open and Tina and Steve stood on the threshold looking in.

Dorothy got quickly to her feet. 'What a surprise,' she exclaimed.

'That's what it was meant to be.' Steve had his arm tightly round Tina's shoulders. 'I didn't dare say a thing until I saw her with my own eyes.'

Looking very poised and in control of herself Tina went up to Dorothy, hand outstretched.

'Hello,' she said.

'Hi,' said Dorothy, still feeling rather shocked, took her hand and shook it.

Tina turned to the crib, but seemed loth to go too near until Steve came up to her again and put his arm round her waist.

'Go on,' he said. 'She's lovely. She's ours.'

'Perhaps I'd better leave you alone,' Dorothy whispered tactfully.

'That might be nice,' Steve murmured turning to her and then in a low voice, 'Do you know where Louise is?'

'I think she's gone to her cottage to check for burst pipes.'

'Perhaps if you saw her you'd tell her Tina is

home.'

'Don't you think you'd better do that yourself, Steve?' Dorothy said rather severely and left the room, still under the influence of shock, fearful as to what would happen when Louise found out that the woman she thought gone for ever had returned.

* * *

As the door shut after Dorothy, Tina moved closer to Steve and took his hand.

'I'm scared,' she said.

'Don't be.' He gently pushed her towards the crib.

'But I am.' Tina still held back. 'I've behaved so badly. Left you with so much.'

'The main thing now,' Steve said reassuringly, 'is that you're back and you're going to stay here.'

'And Louise?'

'Together we can cope with Louise.'

He gently drew Tina towards the crib and pulled back baby's blanket so that her mother could take a peek at her. Baby, just five-weeks old, was sound asleep, her cheeks pink, her rosebud mouth looking a little wistful, even in sleep.

'Isn't she beautiful?' Steve said standing back.

'Oh dear,' Tina put a hand to her eyes and started to cry, 'I didn't mean it to be like this, but yes she is . . . not what I expected, not wrinkly or red. Just perfect.'

'And she is *our* baby!' Steve's arm fastened tightly round her again. 'Not Louise's but ours.'

For some moments they stood gazing at the crib as if they couldn't believe that what lay there they had created between them.

213

'Pick her up,' Steve said at last, gently nudging her forward.

'Oh, but . . .' Still Tina held back.

'Go on. She won't break. She already weighs eleven and a half pounds.'

Tina leaned forward and then rather clumsily and inexpertly tried to pick up baby who opened her eyes, broke into a smile and began to wave her fists in the air with excitement.

Succeeding in her task Tina tightly clutched the smiling baby to her breast. 'Oh, darling,' she murmured, holding her very tight, 'I do love you.'

*   *   *

The four sitting later round the lunch table seemed very stiff and formal.

'Have some more potatoes,' Steve passed the dish to Louise who shook her head.

'I'm not really hungry, but thanks,' she said.

'I suppose you are a little shocked.' Tina looked at her sympathetically.

Louise nodded. 'Steve should have told me instead of leaving it to Dorothy.'

Dorothy, who had endured a good two hours of hell, could not have agreed more.

As it was she had caught Louise on her way into the house and had first forewarned her and then put up with a torrent of tears, recriminations and verbal abuse.

Now Louise seemed remarkably calm. When she had finally emerged from her room and met Tina she even kissed her on the cheek and said 'welcome home', a gesture which seemed to surprise Tina too. Perhaps she had taken one of her pills?

214

Steve was a coward, Dorothy thought, but maybe most men were, though it was difficult to think of Buddy even landing himself in a situation like this, never mind coping with it. How was it that some people were prone to disasters that others seemed to avoid? People in extraordinary circumstances did extraordinary things and showed aspects of their characters you would never have dreamt of.

However, in the course of the meal, Louise, obviously tense, said very little and though she left most of it on her plate she seemed to be continually picking at her food.

'We're awfully grateful to you Louise.' Tina at last found words to break the awkward silence. 'We do want you to know that, and that you will always be part of our lives . . . and baby's.'

'Haven't you decided on a name yet?' Louise forced herself to try and sound casual.

'Not yet,' Steve replied. 'We thought we might keep "baby" as that's what we've called her for so long,' he added jokingly.

'Waiting for Tina to come back I suppose?' Louise's tone rose an octave.

'Well, I hoped . . . yes, I suppose I was.'

'How about Louise? That's a nice name.'

Silence fell once more, a tense, rather threatening silence.

'We'll have to think about it,' Tina's voice was a little faint.

'Or don't you want her to be lumbered with her mother's name?'

'Louise,' Steve said sharply, 'you are not her mother. How many times do you have to be told that?'

'Without me she wouldn't be *here*,' Louise

215

shouted. 'I fed her from my body. I felt her grow, move about. I fucking well gave birth to her. If *that's* not a mother can you tell me what is?'

And then she rose from the table and rushed from the room while the three left behind gazed at one another in horror.

'Dorothy, you better go after her,' Steve said.

'No, I think this time it *should* be you, Steve,' Dorothy said calmly putting her knife and fork together. 'You should have warned her and you didn't. It was wrong of you.'

'I felt it was the best thing to do,' Steve said earnestly. 'Honestly I did. Just for her to see Tina and me together. To know that all her emotions were fantasy. There was never going to be an easy way to tell Louise.'

'I suppose not. But still I think it could have been better handled. It's no use playing games. Louise is a very disturbed person. She's been through a lot. Who knows what she might do to herself?'

'Frankly,' Tina said calmly, 'I think you should give her time to control herself. It is bound to be difficult for Louise, and if we spend our time running after her whenever she has a tantrum there'll be no end to it.'

*   *   *

Louise ran helter-skelter along the path she'd walked along so blithely and cheerfully just that morning when she was thinking of snowdrops and crocuses and a life together with Steve. That very morning she'd talked to Buddy about getting married and having children.

216

Parts of the path were covered with slush, but she didn't care if she slipped or not. She didn't care if she cracked her head open and died.

She wanted to die.

The sight of Tina coming through that door with Steve behind her, both wreathed in smiles, had brought almost unbearable pain. She closed her eyes as she ran, in torment at the memory. It was just unimaginable.

She got to the door of the cottage, fumbled with her key and let herself in.

Lunch had been late and it was almost dark in the cottage. The fire lit that morning had long since gone out. Louise slumped into a chair and stared at the embers, which seemed to epitomise her life; everything turned to ashes.

Feeling desperately tired she almost crawled up the stairs and for a long time lay on her bed waiting for someone to come and tell her that she mattered. They would seek her out, afraid she'd do herself in.

But an hour passed and no one came. No one did care at all about her. She was expendable. She'd done her job.

It was almost dark when she got up and went into the bathroom searching for a packet of tablets in the cabinet, then reading the instructions; not more than eight to be taken in every twenty-four hours.

She went down to the kitchen, found a tumbler, filled it with water and took eight of the tablets straightaway. Then she got a knife out of the kitchen drawer just in case the tablets failed to work.

Slowly she went upstairs, sat on her bed and

took more tablets until the packet was almost empty. Then, as she started to feel groggy, she began to hack away at her wrists with a very sharp knife.

*   *   *

Steve walked along the path to Louise's cottage aware of a deep feeling of foreboding. She had not been back to her room and no one had seen her around the grounds. Even Tina had begun to be apprehensive and urged him to go and find her. Now it was early evening, quite dark and he quickened his steps as he came in sight of the cottage. But there were no lights on and his first reaction was one of relief. However, as he tried the door and found it open that relief changed to apprehension again. He entered the sitting room and switched on the light, saw her coat on the chair and heard the sound of running water from the kitchen. He went in and turned off the tap, looked around, saw nothing amiss and then returned to the sitting room and stood at the bottom of the stairs.

'Louise,' he called, 'are you there?'

There was no reply and he went up the stairs two at a time and stood at the top looking into her room. From the light downstairs he could just see her figure outlined on the bed, one arm hanging limply down.

'Oh, Louise,' he cried, running to her side, *'what have you done?'*

*   *   *

The clinic had once been a stately home set in glorious countryside in Devon, surrounded by woods and with a lake upon which two swans glided majestically. It was primarily for the treatment of addiction to drugs or alcohol, but took other psychiatric cases relevant to the methods offered at the clinic, particularly those connected with obsessional behaviour.

The head of the clinic was Dr Sam Costello, a man in his forties who dressed in jeans and a sweater and was on first name terms with his patients. He had a house in the grounds where he lived with his pretty wife and a young family, and patients as well as staff were encouraged to drop in for tea and enjoy the informal atmosphere that he and his wife created there. She was also a therapist who worked at the clinic.

Louise was admitted to the clinic following her discharge from hospital. It was privately run and Steve had offered to pay all costs. A few weeks after Louise was admitted he had a letter from Sam asking to see him and suggesting he came to his house so that Louise would not know of his presence.

Steve liked Sam and the cosy informal atmosphere he managed to create. They stood chatting in the kitchen while Sam made tea in mugs and then they went back to the sitting room and sat in comfortable armchairs in front of a blazing fire.

Sam was a large man with curly black hair and wore thick, heavy rimmed glasses.

'I like Louise,' Sam said. 'I think we get on. When she first came she was very depressed so I treated the depression, and now she is beginning to come out of it.'

'That's good,' Steve said. 'I feel very bad . . .'

'There is no need for you to feel bad. There is a psychiatric condition named after the French doctor who identified it: de Clarembault. I don't suppose the details particularly interest you. It is a condition whereby the afflicted person is not only obsessively in love with another person, but thinks that person returns the love. They are not aware they are mentally ill.'

'But I never encouraged Louise,' Steve said.

'I believe you.' The doctor sat back. 'However, they do not, or cannot, see this and take every kind gesture as a sign of reciprocal love, even a bunch of flowers or a box of chocolates can assume a meaning the donor never intended.'

'That's just . . .' Steve began, and once more Sam held up his hand.

'I know, she has told me all about it. She thinks that your wife came between you and her, and it is my task to try and persuade her that that was not the case. I quite believe that you did not return her affection in the way she interpreted it. Louise exhibits all the classic symptoms of de Clarembosis and because the patient is so convinced he or she is right, and believes nothing is wrong with them, it is very difficult to treat. However,' he reached for his mug and finished his tea, 'I feel Louise is a borderline case. She has been obsessed, no doubt of that, and there was the unfortunate matter of the baby. That is an added complication. However, she appears to feel little real affection for the baby which quite surprised her. She felt that the baby in fact came between you and her. Her case, of course, was further complicated by her depression and the attempt to kill herself. As it is, a large quantity of paracetamol can seriously damage the liver. She took a vast quantity which could have resulted in death. The wounds to her wrists were also quite deep. She is lucky to be alive. At first she didn't think so, but now I think she does. But it was not a mere cry for help, but a serious attempt to do herself in.'

'Louise is a likeable and intelligent woman who has had a very hard time.' Sam gazed severely across at Steve. 'How is the baby?'

'She is a lovely baby. Very well. My wife is smitten with her. It seems dreadful that we are so happy, whereas poor Louise . . .'

'"Poor Louise" will be alright, with time,' the doctor said. 'I can't guarantee she will recover completely, but the prognosis is reasonable. The thing is,' Sam glanced anxiously at his watch, 'I don't think you and she should meet again for a long time. She accepts this, but I understand she has a home near you and I wondered if there was anywhere else she could go when she is discharged?'

Steve looked perplexed. 'Well, I can't at the moment think of anywhere.'

'Give it some thought.' Sam got up. 'I have a case conference in ten minutes. By the way is there any limit as to how long she can stay here? I understand you're taking care of the bill. Normally we like to detain patients no longer than six weeks or so, but Louise may need a little more time.'

'No limit at all,' Steve said expansively. 'It's the least we can do. I feel a deep responsibility for my part in ruining that young woman's life.'

*　　　*　　　*

221

Louise felt that her time at the clinic, which at first she had deeply resented, had been like rediscovering her life. There was little regimentation and for a long time they left her alone, attending meals when she felt like it and, except for long sessions with Sam and another therapist, she avoided the company of her fellow patients.

They were mostly young people like herself, sometimes younger, and there were several older patients who had abused drugs or alcohol all their lives.

She would meet them in the hall, in the dining room and sometimes walking around the grounds, but she avoided any closeness until Sam pointed out that it was her relative isolation at Poynton which may have contributed to her obsession with Steve. She was essentially a loner. For a long time she maintained that Steve had reciprocated her affection. Why, after all, had he wanted her to have his baby?

Gradually Louise got to know some people better, particularly a young woman called Marcia who had been a heroin addict since she was a teenager and had come close to death. She too had tried to end her life and she persuaded Louise that talking about things in a group of people who had all been through various traumas in their lives was beneficial.

There was always an expert counsellor in attendance and although sessions sometimes ended in tears, Louise began regularly to attend these groups and to benefit from them. She was not condemned, she could play out her resentment, often bitterness; no one called her foolish or silly to feel as she had about Steve, but it did seem unrealistic the more she tried to understand it.

She had never known her father who had died when she was a baby and Steve, an older man, had combined the attributes of father and, for her, would-be lover. She had to admit the fact that there never had been intimacy between them, except in her imagination when she was implanted with the embryo of Steve and his wife. It was rather shaming to have to confess that.

Louise gradually stopped thinking that everyone was wrong and she was right. She began not only to enjoy the therapy groups but to socialise more. Her drugs were cut down and she became less dependent on them.

One fine day in early spring she was sitting with a group on rugs on the lawn. They were taking advantage of the mild weather to work out of doors. The daffodils clustered round the base of the tree, and a breeze ruffled the waters of the little lake just below them. White clouds like fluffy cottonwool balls scudded across the blue sky.

'I thought that when the daffodils came out Steve and I would be together,' Louise said with a lump in her throat. 'I never thought I'd be here.'

There was silence as the group members seemed to empathise with her grief. A man called Charles put his arm round her neck. Charles had had a severe drugs and alcohol problem and he, Marcia, Louise and another man called Darren spent a lot of time in each other's company. It was not a sexual thing. It was a friendship thing.

Just at that moment Louise looked up and saw a figure approaching across the lawn. Recognising it

223

she jumped up, exclaiming 'Dorothy!' Excitedly she turned to her companions.

'Excuse me. Someone has come to see me!'

Dorothy was the first outside visitor Louise had had and the therapy group seemed to share her pleasure. Most of them had husbands, wives, partners, parents or other close friends or relatives who came to see them, but Louise had never had anyone, which seemed to emphasise how lonely she had been. This group had now become her family.

Louise ran across to Dorothy and the two women embraced.

'So *good* to see you,' Louise began.

'Sorry I didn't come before.'

'No need.' Louise eagerly led her across to a bench. 'I was horribly depressed. I didn't want to see anyone.'

'Better now?' Dorothy looked at her hopefully.

'Much,' Louise gestured in the direction of the group near the tree who were proceeding with their discussions without her. 'They're a great bunch of people.'

'Has it been of any help,' Dorothy asked, 'being here?'

'Tremendous help. You see, we're all in the same boat. Oh, not the *same*, but we've all had terrible problems. And we are encouraged and able to talk about them.' Louise paused. 'How is . . . everyone. Steve?'

'All well. They send their love and I've left a few bits and pieces for you at reception.'

'And does the baby have a name yet?'

Dorothy had been dreading this question but Louise appeared very matter of fact.

'They've called her Judith.'

Louise nodded approvingly. 'Judith is a nice name. You know, from where I am now it all seems to have happened such a long time ago. Yet only a year ago I was expecting . . . well, I still think of her as "baby". It will be very hard to return to it all. In fact, Sam, who is the director of the clinic, thinks when I am ready for discharge I should go away for a while.'

'Oh, I *agree*,' Dorothy said enthusiastically. 'And in that connection Steve had an idea. He has bought this vineyard in Australia, quite a large one, and he wondered if you'd like to go and work in the shop, when you're ready of course. It's a big shop selling wine and souvenirs.'

'Oh, Steve had that idea already had he?' Louise's tone turned sarcastic. 'Anxious to get rid of me I expect.'

Dorothy put a hand on her arm. 'Please don't jump to conclusions. Steve is anxious to *help* you I think. Can't you try and see it that way?'

*   *   *

After Dorothy had gone Louise didn't return to the group but went off to her room and lay on the bed. She thought about Australia and working in the vineyard shop and it had a certain appeal. In fact it seemed quite exciting.

The following day she discussed it with Sam over tea at his house. Sam had also heard from Steve and thought it was a good idea.

'We also have support groups in Australia if you ever feel you need help.'

'Does this mean I'll never see Steve again?'

'Not   necessarily.'   Sam   looked   at   her

thoughtfully. 'One day you might be ready for it, or you might feel you don't want to. You have your home at Poynton and you can come back whenever you want. I suggest you give Australia a try because I think you're very nearly ready to be discharged.' He regarded her affectionately. 'You've made great progress, you know Louise. I think you've gained a lot of insight you didn't have before. You've done a good job. Now you must forgive yourself, be kind to yourself and try and get as much out of life as you can.'

*   *   *

Steve opened the last of his post and gasped when he saw the size of the bill. The good news, however, was that Louise wanted to go to Australia and work in the vineyard shop. Dr Costello wondered if Steve would be prepared to bear all the expense? It had already amounted to thousands.

He looked out of the window to the new building rising from the ground, already half built. The builders had made tremendous progress when they started again after all the snow had gone. The hotel complex might be ready by next spring. The shop had reopened at Easter and Tina, having learned her lessons as well from the past, was careful not to overstock. Duncan was full of plans for extending the greenhouses and introducing new plant varieties. Everything had started to go right after Tina returned.

Steve felt very happy, very blessed. Very lucky, in fact. He went out of his study to look for Tina and found her with Judith who was sitting in her baby chair being fed with mashed banana by her mother, most of it running down her face, and both of them seeming vastly amused by it. She waved her spoon when she saw her father who stooped and first kissed her on the head, then Tina.

'You both have golden curls,' he murmured. 'I've had a letter from the clinic. *And* a bill.' He raised his eyes heavenwards.

'Oh *tell*,' Tina said, taking the spoon from Judith and putting it in the mashed banana again.

'Well it's costing a fortune, but she is willing to go to Australia. In fact, quite excited about it. I must say they've done an amazing job. Sam Costello says she is full of beans and practically off medication. He says they have support groups in Australia who follow the same methods if she should ever need help again.'

'We must do all we can for Louise,' Tina said earnestly. 'Some people pay a fortune to have a baby and . . . well . . . Louise was never greedy. She just wanted love. She never asked for money did she?'

Steve shook his head. 'However, I think at this rate I'm going to be keeping Louise for the rest of her life.'

'Well, it's worth doing.' Tina gazed into the blue eyes of the child Louise had borne for them, yet who was like her, not the surrogate.

Steve looked at his wife with admiration. 'You're amazingly generous, seeing that you disliked her so much.'

'It's just that I feel I have everything, and poor Louise has nothing. She's given us so much happiness, Steve. For that we must be grateful and try to forget about the rest.'

The airport was crowded and Louise suddenly felt apprehensive. Beside her were Buddy and Dorothy who had come all the way to see her off.

Buddy thought that Louise looked like a different person, or rather, more like the one he had first known and imagined himself in love with. She looked well and had an air of confidence, despite her fears about such a long journey. Everything had been taken care of at the other end and she would be met at the airport and driven to her new home.

'Steve and Tina send their love,' Dorothy said. 'Best wishes and all that.'

'Thanks.' Louise looked thoughtful. 'I expected that Steve might just possibly have come to see me off?'

'Would you *really* have wanted him to?' Dorothy looked at her searchingly.

'Perhaps not. Not yet.' Louise gave a sly smile. 'Anyway, Sam would not have approved.' She picked up her bag as the tannoy announced the departure of her plane.

Now her apprehension deepened. Momentarily she appeared to hesitate. She was, after all, flying off into the unknown. It was a long, long way. Dorothy seized hold of her arm and pushed her gently towards the gate. 'Hurry or you'll miss the plane.'

Louise suddenly threw her arms round Dorothy, kissed her on both cheeks and then did the same to Buddy. She stood back and looked at him.

'You're a great guy,' she said. 'I should have grabbed you while I had the chance. Be happy.'

'And you.' Buddy felt almost on the verge of tears. '*You* be happy too.'

'I shall be,' Louise said cheerily taking up her case again. 'Don't worry.'

'Be sure to write,' Dorothy called out as Louise showed her passport at the gate, then held up her hand and passed out of sight.

*   *   *

As the plane lifted into the sky, Louise looked through the window at the tiny specks upon the ground and thought how good of Dorothy and Buddy to come all that way to see her. As the plane flew higher and the ground receded she experienced a sense of elation, of freedom as well as fear of the unknown. Now that she was on her way a sense of calm, of excitement about the future seemed to settle on her.

There was always a line to Sam and help in Australia if she needed it. After all, the vineyard belonged to Steve, so she was not cutting off all connection with him.

Unfastening her seatbelt she rested her head back against the seat and closed her eyes.

Certainly a new world awaited her. She supposed, though, that she would think of Steve from time to time, and from time to time she would miss him.

After all, a bond once formed could never be broken.

Chivers Large Print Direct

If you have enjoyed this Large Print book and would like to build up your own collection of Large Print books and have them delivered direct to your door, please contact **Chivers Large Print Direct**.

Chivers Large Print Direct offers you a full service:

✰ **Created to support your local library**

✰ **Delivery direct to your door**

✰ **Easy-to-read type and attractively bound**

✰ **The very best authors**

✰ **Special low prices**

For further details either call Customer Services on 01225 443400 or write to us at

Chivers Large Print Direct
FREEPOST (BA 1686/1)
Bath
BA1 3QZ